FALLING FOR HER
FRENCH TYCOON

FALLING FOR HER FRENCH TYCOON

REBECCA WINTERS

MILLS & BOON

First published in Great Britain 2020
by Mills & Boon, an imprint of HarperCollins*Publishers*
1 London Bridge Street, London, SE1 9GF

Large Print edition 2020

© 2020 Rebecca Winters

ISBN: 978-0-263-08462-7

MIX
Paper from
responsible sources
FSC
www.fsc.org
FSC˚ C007454

This book is produced from independently certified FSC™ paper to ensure responsible forest management. For more information visit www.harpercollins.co.uk/green.

Printed and bound in Great Britain
by CPI Group (UK) Ltd, Croydon, CR0 4YY

Once again I turn to my oldest son, whom I often call Guillaume, because he's a Francophile like his *maman* and fluent in their beautiful language. Turning to him for information about my favorite place on earth is better than any book. His knowledge continues to stun me. We have the most marvelous conversations and I learn so much. How I love him!

PROLOGUE

July 31

NATHALIE FOURNIER RANG Claire Rolon, the best friend of Nathalie's deceased stepsister, Antoinette. The friendship between the three of them went back to childhood.

"Claire?"

"Nathalie! I'm so glad you called! It's been ages."

"Way too long. I'm thrilled you answered. Do you have a minute?"

"Yes. Robert is upstairs playing with the baby while I finish the dishes. Go ahead."

She took a deep breath. "I know Antoinette would have confided in you before she got pregnant two and a half years ago. Is there anything you can tell me about her lover who disappeared on her without explanation? Our family didn't know she'd even been involved with someone until the doctor said she was pregnant. By then she'd sunk into a deep depression."

"Your stepsister was very secretive."

"So secretive she never spoke his name to us and as she died from infection ten days after her baby was born, we still don't know who his father is," Nathalie lamented. "Now little Alain is fifteen months old and I'm taking the steps to legally adopt him. Before I do, though, I need to try to find his father."

"You're kidding! How could you possibly do that?"

"Hopefully with a little information you could provide." Nathalie gripped the phone tighter. "You probably think I'm crazy."

"Of course I don't."

"You were the closest person to her, Claire. If she said anything, it would have been to you. Any clue you could give me would help. Did she let it slip where or how she met him?"

"She did say he worked at the Fontesquieu vineyard."

Her heart raced. "You're certain of that?"

The Fontesquieu vineyards near Vence, France, were one of the largest and most prestigious, producing the legendary rosé wines of Provence. The land had been deeded to them by royalty centuries ago, and the most coveted vineyard in all Provence was currently run by a titled billionaire. She'd heard stories about the vineyard all her life.

"Yes. Apparently they met at a bistro in Vence where a lot of the vineyard workers from the Fontesquieu estate hang out during the harvest."

"Do you remember the name of it?" Nathalie cried, encouraged by what she'd just learned.

"It was unusual. The Guingot, or some such name, but I don't imagine he would be at that vineyard after all this time. I wish there was something more concrete to tell you. It's not much to go on. I'm so sorry. I think you'll need a miracle."

"Don't be sorry, Claire! The vineyard is the place where I'm going to start looking. One more thing. Did she say what he looked like?"

"Unfortunately not. Only that he was a Provencal and the only man she would ever love."

That meant he'd been a local Frenchman, probably dark haired and eyed.

"You've given me more information than I could have hoped for. Thank you with all my heart."

"Good luck. Let me know if you learn anything."

"I will. You're such a good friend. Thank you for being so honest with me. I know she swore you to secrecy."

"She did, but it's been a long time since then. For Alain's sake it would be wonderful if you're successful."

"Wouldn't it? Talk to you soon."

Nathalie hung up, deep in thought.

At the beginning of the summer, Nathalie had broken up with the man she'd thought she might marry. Guy couldn't handle her bringing Alain into their marriage—he wanted his own child with her.

That's when she'd told him she probably couldn't have children. When she'd explained about having primary ovarian insufficiency, he couldn't handle that news. Guy had said he'd wanted to marry her, but he'd refused to consider adopting Alain. Because she wanted her nephew more than anything, it became clear that marriage was out of the question.

Alain meant everything to her.

CHAPTER ONE

August 31

ADRENALINE GUSHED THROUGH Nathalie as she sped toward the Fontesquieu vineyards of Vence—queen of the cities of the French Riviera, in her opinion. They stretched eye to eye above the blue Mediterranean, row after row of immaculately tended *terroirs* with their healthy grape vines dotting the undulating green hills and summits.

The August afternoon sun had ripened the luscious grapes, filling the air with a sweet, fruity smell as she neared the Fontesquieu estate with its enormous seventeenth-century chateau, rumored to contain twenty-two bedrooms. It reminded her of the book *My Mother's Castle*, made famous by the French author and filmmaker Marcel Pagnol. He'd been born in Provence too and had written some of her favorite books about his childhood memories.

But the Pagnol family's quaint little vacation home in Provence couldn't compare to the one she could see out the window of her trusty old Peugeot. The magnificent chateau had always been closed to the public, but the estate drew artists and tourists from all over the world.

Nathalie couldn't imagine the wealth of a family like the Fontesquieux. She'd been born in Provence and had passed by the vineyard many times, but she'd never enjoyed its scenery more than this afternoon.

With pounding heart, she followed the signs posted to find the tent set up for people seeking temporary work grape picking. After planning this since her talk with Claire a month ago, the day had come for her to get a job that would last only the three weeks of the grape harvest. In that amount of time, she hoped to find the man who had fathered her nephew, Alain, if he was still there. But as Claire had said, it would take a miracle.

When she reached the nearby mobile home park she'd visited earlier in the week, she parked and walked down the road toward a line of people waiting outside the tent in the distance.

Before entering, a man—probably early twenties—with dark blond hair handed everyone an application to fill out. He also gave them a list of items they would need if they were eventually hired. She put that list in her purse and sat down at a small table to fill out the form before getting in line. He eyed her with obvious male interest before it was her turn to enter the tent.

The line moved slowly until there was only one person in front of her being interviewed. That's when she saw the man vetting everyone and stifled a gasp. She wished she had a better description of Alain's father. All she had to go on was that he was a Provencal, which meant dark haired and dark eyed. The man sitting there certainly filled that description, but it could be a coincidence. Was it possible she'd found him?

The breathtaking, late-twenties-looking male could easily be the heartthrob Antoinette had fallen for! Her darling stepsister's now sixteen-month-old child possessed this man's square chin and black hair. He had the same type of build and olive skin.

Thousands of Frenchmen claimed those same qualifications, but this one's piercing black eyes had a distinct look that reminded her so much of her little nephew, Nathalie was astonished. To think, it might be Alain's father sitting there not ten feet away interviewing would-be grape pickers. By applying for this job, she could have found him!

According to one of the people in line, hundreds of workers had already been hired during the week. Today represented the last group seeking temporary employment.

"Prochain?" he said in a deep voice that reached her insides.

Nathalie's heartbeat sped up as she realized she was next in line and needed to follow through. She moved forward to sit opposite him on a chair beneath the tent. The heat of the sun had made the interior uncomfortably warm.

Though he was seated, she could tell he was a tall man, lean in that appealing masculine way. He wore a white shirt with the sleeves pushed to the elbows and as he took the application from her, she noticed a small, pale, café-au-lait birthmark on his underarm beneath the elbow. She had to stifle another gasp because the back of Alain's right calf had the same birthmark.

Maybe it was a coincidence. Millions of people had them, but this was just one more bit of evidence to convince her he could be Alain's father.

Nathalie noticed that he wore a watch and no rings, but that didn't mean he wasn't married. His nails were immaculate. When he looked up, their eyes met and her breath caught.

Heat crept into her cheeks as she got lost in his intense gaze. They were both taking measure of each other while she waited for him to say something. He couldn't have recognized her as Antoinette's stepsister. Nathalie was a blonde. Her stepsister had been a brunette. They came from different sets of parents with different last names.

His virile male beauty stunned her. Her stepsister, who'd been two years older than Nathalie, would have taken one look at him and that would have been it! How well Nathalie understood the instant attraction. She couldn't look away.

He continued to study her features. "Mademoiselle Fournier? I see here you've had no experience as a *vendangeuse.*"

"That's right. I didn't know that was a prerequisite."

"It's not, but it's hard labor, seasonal, and the pay isn't that great. Why would a pharmacist from La Gaude apply to do entry-level work like this?" La Gaude, France, was a town a fifteen-minute drive from Vence along the Côte d'Azur, the playground of the world's rich and famous.

She felt those black all-seeing eyes travel over her with a thoroughness that caused her to tremble, and she looked down. He was so gorgeous she was in danger of forgetting why she'd come. For her little nephew's sake, it was vital Nathalie pull this off. She needed to think fast.

"I've lived in Provence all my life and thought that for once I'd use my vacation time to find out what it's like to work in a vineyard as world renowned as this one."

On their website she'd seen one photo of the Duc Armand de Fontesquieu, the gray-haired, eighty-year-old patriarch and CEO. She'd seen no other pictures and realized they had to be a very private family.

Though many vineyards used machinery, some vintners—like the vastly wealthy Fontesquieu family with their many *terroirs*—also hired pickers called *coupeurs*, plus collectors and sorters for the grape harvest *vendange*. It lasted for the first three weeks of September. She'd done her homework.

After a slight pause, he spoke. "You do realize that we have no accommodations for you here."

She raised her eyes to him again. With that comment, she sensed he didn't believe her reason for wanting the temporary work.

Though it was this man's job to vet would-be workers, she sensed he had reservations about her. Obviously the "no previous vineyard work" written on the form bothered him. Naturally anyone could apply for grape picking, but their vineyard would welcome those with experience.

"Yes. That's why I've rented a mobile home at the park down the road from here." Actually she'd come two days ago to put a hold on one until she knew the outcome of this interview.

He gave her a level stare. "Keep in mind you'll have an hour for lunch and quit at four thirty. If you're still interested in working here by Monday morning, report to the tent at six o'clock and the assistant vineyard manager will let you know if you've been hired."

It was all up to this man who would have the weekend to check out her references. He spoke with authority. There was an aura of sophistication about him that let her know he had a position of importance at Fontesquieux and had likely worked here long enough to have met Antoinette at the bistro.

"*Merci*, monsieur." She got up, aware of him watching her as she walked past the people standing in line, and left the tent. The younger man outside giving out applications flashed her a smile, but she looked away and headed for her car, not wanting to encourage him.

When she got behind the wheel, she was still feeling shaky from all the sensations bombarding her. It might be a long shot, but now that she suspected she'd met the man who could be Alain's father, she'd do everything possible to get to know him. When she sensed it was the right moment, she'd show him photos of Antoinette and Alain, including the birthmark. If he was the father, she couldn't imagine him not wanting to see his child.

Of course, if she didn't get hired, then she needed to find innovative ways to cross paths with him, starting tonight. She planned to seek out dinner at the bistro Claire had told her about. Maybe *he'd* be there... Just imagining his handsome features left her breathless.

Having finished the interviews, Dominic Laurent Fontesquieu stopped in the midst of fastening his briefcase full of applications. He couldn't resist taking another look at the Fournier application.

The woman with translucent green eyes and natural silvery blond hair had robbed him of breath. Her deportment and stunning beauty had captivated him. As Dominic studied the particulars on her application, her image swam before him again.

Age: twenty-seven.
Home address: La Gaude.

Cell phone...

Email address...

Employed full time at La Metropole Pharmacy.

Driver's license.

Own car.

Bank account.

Covered by social insurance.

Degree in pharmacology from Sophie Antipolis University in Nice.

No experience picking grapes.

He tapped the paper against his jaw. What was missing here? Only everything else about her life that might answer the question of what prompted her to apply for this temporary work.

This mysterious, gorgeous, educated woman suddenly appears at the vineyard out of nowhere, wanting to know what it's like to help with the harvest for a few weeks?

Dominic didn't buy it for a second. He put the application in the briefcase with the others before leaving the tent, unable to get her off his mind. He was so attracted to her, it shocked him.

Vetting would-be workers was one of his brother Etienne's jobs as director of the vineyard so he usually oversaw the vendange hiring. But he'd been struck down by a nasty flu bug for the better part of a week and their grandfather Armand had rung Dominic's apartment in the south wing of the chateau and demanded that he fill in for his brother.

Little had Dominic known that the most beautiful woman he'd ever laid eyes on in his life would be among the applicants. He'd wanted to catch up with her after she'd left and take her to dinner to get to know her better. But that had been impossible when other people needed to be interviewed.

Frustrated, he headed for his office in a building on the estate behind the chateau. He left the applications for his assistant, Theo, to deal with until Etienne recovered and drove the short distance to the chateau. Once he reached his apartment, he took a quick shower to cool off.

Until today he'd never found a woman whose looks turned him inside out in just one short meeting. In fact he'd doubted if such a woman even existed. But this afternoon, a pair of translucent green eyes had caught him completely off guard.

Throughout the eleven years he'd been away from home in Paris, he'd enjoyed several intimate relationships with beautiful women. But he'd never experienced this instant, intense, earthy kind of attraction to a woman, not even when he'd been a teenager. And he sure as hell hadn't seen a woman like her show up for work at the vineyard before.

After putting on a robe, he went to the kitchen to make himself a sandwich. While he ate, he phoned Etienne with an update and told him not to worry, Dominic would continue to cover for him and told him to get better. After hanging up, he needed a distraction. He turned on the TV to watch the news, but nothing helped get his mind off Nathalie Fournier.

She was on some kind of mission. He was

certain of it. Though a pharmacist, maybe she had an ambitious streak and did freelancing undercover for a newspaper or a wine industry magazine to make extra money.

He wished his cousin Raoul was home so they could talk. They were closer than brothers and always confided in each other. But Raoul and his father, Matthieu, the comptroller of the company, were in Saint Tropez at a vintners' conference and they wouldn't be back until Sunday night.

Any conversation would have to wait until Monday. *And then what, Dominic?*

Maybe some politician was paying a lot of money for her to get an exclusive on the vineyard. Was it hoped that her digging would turn up something she could expose concerning the migrants who worked at the Fontesquieu vineyard? No one would suspect her under the guise of a pharmacist, of all things.

He supposed anything was possible and didn't like what he was thinking. Half a dozen ideas of what she might be up to percolated in his mind, as his domineering grandfather was always guarding against trespassers.

Dominic's thoughts turned to his autocratic grandfather who'd been born with a *divine right of kings* syndrome. He felt a bleak expression cross over his features. The austere man's dictatorial personality had forced the whole family to live under his thumb. He'd forced arranged marriages for all his six sons and daughters, and insisted they all live and work together at the massive chateau, determined to keep it all in the family.

Armand had screwed up more lives than Dominic dared count. Under his tutelage, Dominic's own father and mother, Gaston and Vivienne, had put unbearable pressure on him and his siblings to marry certain moneyed, elite people they'd picked out for them. At eighteen, Dominic had refused to be told what to do.

No one in the family—including his parents—had had a good or happy marriage, souring Dominic's taste for the institution. Early on he'd made up his mind to study business and carve out his own future. It had been imperative he get away from the family dynamics to survive. His dreams had gone far beyond being a vintner and he'd left home for Paris under the threat of being disinherited, but he hadn't cared.

He'd begged his brother to go with him, but Etienne had held back, too unsure to challenge their father and grandfather. Their older sister, Quinette, had already been married off.

Ultimately, Etienne stayed and Dominic had left alone, putting himself through college. After graduation he'd studied investment banking in Paris and, in time, he'd worked for a firm there where he'd made a considerable fortune in investments, coming home only for vacations and various events.

He would have stayed there permanently, but four months ago he'd received a frantic call from his mother that his father was seriously ill with pneumonia and might die.

Dominic had intended to return to Vence only temporarily but his grandfather immediately insisted Dominic take over his father's position as funds manager while the older man was ill.

Still hesitant to remain in Vence, it was Raoul, now vice president in charge of marketing and sales for the Fontesquieu Corporation, who'd been the one to beg Dominic to take the job and not go back to Paris.

The two of them had been best friends growing up, always watching out for one another. Over the years they'd always stayed in touch, Raoul visiting Paris when he could. In the end, Dominic hadn't been able to refuse Raoul and so had stayed on while his father was recovering.

He was no fool though. Ever since his return, he'd known his grandfather had an ulterior motive in wanting Dominic to take over the management of funds. Because of a bad year of frost and rain two years ago, the vineyards in France had suffered severe financial losses and even their family had been impacted despite their assets in other businesses.

Dominic knew his father and grandfather were plotting for him to marry Corinne Herlot, who'd bring the fabulous Herlot industrial fortune with her. She'd been at several family parties, but he could never be interested and had planned to leave for Paris by the time the harvest was over.

At least that was what he'd intended *until* today when Nathalie Fournier had appeared. Now there was no way in this world could he leave yet...

Nathalie could hear the sound of jazz outside the swinging doors of what turned out to be the Guinguet bistro. There were people going in and out, enjoying the balmy Friday night air with its hint of fruit from the vineyards. She could well understand the lure this atmosphere had held for her stepsister.

Easing past couples, Nathalie walked inside the crowded establishment filled with small round tables and people slow dancing to the music. In the romantic atmosphere, she realized she hadn't had a date since breaking up with Guy three months ago.

It had hurt that he wouldn't want to take on anyone else's child, whether it was Alain or a child they might adopt after marriage. She couldn't imagine a childless union, but knew that adoption wasn't an option for everyone. She'd hoped Guy would be open to it but he couldn't have made his feelings against it clearer.

She'd learned of her condition at the age of twenty. Nathalie had ovulated only once by then. That was seven years ago. Since that time, she'd ovulated only twice. After what had happened with Guy, her natural worry was that any man she would meet in the future might have reservations about adoption, but she couldn't think about that now. Nathalie knew it had been the right decision to stop seeing Guy and didn't regret it.

Her mind kept going over what had happened to Antoinette. Her stepsister had fallen madly in love with a man she'd met in this very bistro. She'd loved him so much she'd had his baby.

Today Nathalie felt certain she'd met her stepsister's lover inside that tent. One look at him and she'd understood the chemistry. Love at first sight, sweeping Antoinette away. But clearly the fire had been only on her stepsister's part because he'd disappeared on her.

He couldn't have known he'd left her pregnant, could he? After meeting him, Nathalie knew he was the kind of man who could have any woman he wanted. Antoinette had likely been a dalliance for a month, then nothing more.

Now that Nathalie had met him, she feared that if he was Alain's father, he wouldn't want anything to do with a baby he hadn't intended to sire. Nathalie was beginning to think this had been a terrible idea and she should leave this whole thing alone. Alain had a surfeit of love from her and his grandmother. That would have to be enough.

"Mademoiselle?"

A man's voice caused Nathalie to turn around. She'd been admiring some of the paintings of the Fontesquieu chateau and gardens adorning the walls.

"Perhaps you remember me?"

She blinked. "Yes. You were the man handing out applications earlier today."

"That's right. When I saw you walk in alone just now, I thought I'd say hello and offer to buy you a drink. My table is right here."

This was probably how it had happened for Antoinette. Her lover had approached her in exactly the same way. Nathalie had to do some fast thinking. If she accepted the invite, she could at least learn the name of the man who had interviewed her. But she wasn't attracted to this man and didn't want him to misunderstand.

"Thank you, but I only came in to look around."

"You can do that right here." He pulled out a bistro chair for her so she would sit down.

Then he took the other seat. "Have you been in here before?"

"Never."

"My name is Paul Cortier, by the way."

"I'm Nathalie Fournier."

"*Eh, bien,* Nathalie, please allow me to order you the specialty of the house, although you may not like it. Guinguet is an acquired taste."

"Guinguet? Like the name of the bistro?"

"*C'est exacte.*" He signaled for a waiter who took their order. "The word comes from the *guinguettes* that were popular drinking places on the outskirts of Paris years ago. They served local sour white wine, a tradition this bistro keeps up."

"Who makes the sour white wine here?"

"The Fontesquieu Vineyards."

"Of course. Your employer."

"That's right. They make enough of it to keep the owner here in business."

"Even though their grapes are red?"

Paul chuckled. "There are lots of secrets about red grapes I'd be happy to explain to you on another occasion. Perhaps on a tour of the winery itself? I'd be happy to arrange to show you personally."

She shook her head. "Thank you, but just so you know, I'm not interested in a relationship with anyone, Paul." It was the truth.

He squinted at her. "At least you're honest."

The waiter brought them each a small goblet of pale white wine. After he walked away, Paul lifted his glass. "Try it and let me know what you think."

Nathalie, who didn't actually like wine, took a sip, then struggled not to make a face.

Paul laughed. "Somehow I knew that would be your reaction. It's not for everyone. But since you'll be helping with the harvest, I thought you'd like a sample. Sort of a christening for you."

She took another sip to please him. "I may not be hired."

"Unless you have a police record, I don't see any problem. Please tell me you don't." He was a charming flirt who never gave up.

She chuckled. "Not as far as I know."

"That's the best news I've had since I handed you an application."

"I guess I'll find out Monday morning if I made the cut. My interview didn't last long since the man saw on the application that I knew nothing about grape picking."

He cocked his head. "Is that true?"

"Yes, but I think it would be interesting to learn."

"It's hard work."

"Ooh. I'm sure there's a great deal to learn and endure." She took one more sip, but knew she could never acquire a taste for it. "Now I hope you don't mind, but I have to get going. When you spoke to me, I had only come in here to take a look around because one of the people in line told me about this place. It was very nice of you to buy me a drink." There was no sign of the striking French god who'd interviewed her earlier.

"I'm sorry you have to go. Let me walk you out."

"That won't be necessary."

"No problem. I'm leaving too." He cleared their way through the crowds and walked her to her car, where she got in.

She spoke to him through the open window. "If I'm hired, we'll probably see each other again."

"I'm planning on it. Otherwise I'll ask my boss why you didn't get the job. He'll go to Dominic for an explanation."

"Dominic?"

"Dominic Fontesquieu. He's one of the family heads who interviewed you earlier today."

What?

"He rarely does any interviewing, but his brother, Etienne Fontesquieu, director of the vineyard, has been ill. If there was a problem with you, Gregoire will get it straightened out with Etienne so you will be hired. You can trust me on that."

"Thank you very much, Paul. *Bonne nuit.*"

CHAPTER TWO

NATHALIE DROVE AWAY with her heart in her throat. Could Alain be the son of Dominic Fontesquieu? A man who came from one of the most prominent, titled families in France?

Had it been an illicit affair on his part that he didn't want getting back to his family? Had he sworn Antoinette to silence because of his name?

Maybe he'd been married and couldn't afford a scandal that would make the news. If he were divorced now, it could explain the lack of a wedding ring. Or maybe he didn't like to wear rings. She wondered if he'd kept his name a secret from Antoinette.

Suffused with more questions than before, Nathalie drove faster than usual, needing answers. Fifteen minutes later, she entered the house and found her mother in the family room watching TV while she worked on some embroidered blocks for a quilt. All was quiet, which meant Alain was asleep.

Nathalie sat down on the couch. "I'm glad you're still up, Maman, because I've got something of vital importance to tell you."

Her mother took one look at her and turned off the TV.

"Please don't be upset with me if I tell you something that might make you angry."

"Why would you say that?"

For the next ten minutes, Nathalie told her about her talk with Claire a month ago and her plan to look for Alain's father. She explained about her visit to the Fontesquieu vineyard to apply for work, and ended by telling her about today's discovery.

"This afternoon I found a man I believe could be Alain's father and learned his name."

Her mother leaned forward. "Good heavens, Nathalie. What do you mean you think you've found him?"

When Nathalie told her what had happened today, her mother jumped to her feet looking startled. "Alain could be a Fontesquieu?"

"Yes. If the man who interviewed me is the one, I can see why Antoinette fell for him. He's...so incredibly attractive, I can't believe it." Nathalie had been mesmerized by him.

"I've never heard you talk this way about a man before."

She drew in a breath. "That's because I've never met one like him in my whole life. It would explain what happened to Antoinette." She cleared her throat. "On the drive back just now, I decided that if I'm hired on Monday, I'll work there long enough to find out his marital status. If he's divorced or single, then I'll approach him. But if he's married and has children, then for the sake of his wife and family, I'm not sure how I'll inform him."

"Oh, Nathalie." Her voice shook. "Darling… You're going to have to be careful without positive proof."

"There *is* proof if you compare the two of them, even without a DNA test. The resemblance is uncanny. And there's something else. Dominic Fontesquieu has the same small birthmark as Alain."

"I'm afraid that still doesn't prove paternity."

"You're right."

Her mother seemed anxious.

"Don't worry, Maman. I promise to talk everything over with you before I make any kind of a move."

"You honestly believe this Dominic could be the one?"

"In my opinion, yes. Just think—if he knew he had a son and wanted him—how wonderful it would be for Alain to get to know at least one of his parents. He's such a treasure, I would think any father worth his salt would give anything to claim him."

"I agree, but I'm afraid to credit any of this because—"

Nathalie got up and hugged her. "Because it would be a dream come true if Alain's father wanted him and they could be united."

Her mother nodded. "But darling, it could be a nightmare if there isn't a good ending to this story."

"I know, Maman. Not every man would welcome that kind of news. I won't do anything until we're in total agreement."

Dominic was already awake at five Monday morning when his phone rang. He checked the caller ID. Something had to be wrong for his brother to call this early.

"Etienne? Have you taken a turn for the worse?"

"*Non, non*, but the doctor won't let me go to work for a few more days. *Desolé*, Dom." His voice still sounded an octave lower than normal.

"I'll be happy to fill in until you're better and will help Gregoire."

"Thanks, brother."

Nothing could have made Dominic happier since he wanted to get to know Mademoiselle Fournier. "Stay in bed and relax. Theo did all the background checks on Friday's applicants and informed Gregoire. No red flags on anyone."

Which meant none on Mademoiselle Fournier, whose image refused to leave his mind. She'd never been in trouble. No parking infractions or car accidents, no warrants out for her arrest. He hadn't really expected anything negative to come up on her but relief had swept through him when he learned she was squeaky clean, even though he still had the feeling she'd come to the vineyard for a hidden reason. He planned to get to the bottom of it.

"That's good considering we need workers," Etienne murmured. "This is a bigger harvest than last year, *Dieu merci*. Such news will make Grand-père happy."

"I'll drive to the tent now."

"Paul will be there to help. Thanks, Dom."

"Au revoir."

After hanging up, Dominic quickly showered and shaved. On his way out the door dressed in jeans and a fresh white shirt, he grabbed a plum and a baguette to hold him over until lunch.

Hurrying to the main garage on the property, he picked one of the trucks rigged with gear to help the workers and headed for the tent at the base of the western *terroirs*. Judging by the temperature outside, it was going to be another hot day, which meant the bulging grapes needed picking now.

Mademoiselle Fournier was in for some hard, menial work. By the end of the harvest he'd discover why she'd really come to the vineyard. With more excitement than he should be feeling, he parked near the tent where Gregoire and Paul were addressing the latest crop of new workers.

Though dressed like the others in rainproof layered clothing and gum shoes to protect themselves from the morning dew, she stood out from everyone else. Her height plus the feminine mold of her body made it impossible for him to look anywhere else.

This morning she'd tied her shimmering hair back at the nape of her neck with a band, revealing high cheekbones and a softly rounded chin. He'd studied the enticing shape of her mouth on Friday and the image had stayed with him all weekend, making him wonder how he'd last until he'd be close to her again.

He parked next to the other two trucks and waited until Gregoire gave final instructions to the workers. One by one they climbed into the truck beds with the aid of ladders. From here they'd be driven to the vineyard needing attention.

At that point Dominic got out of his own truck. He lowered the tailgate and attached his ladder so the last ten workers being ushered by Paul could climb in. He was happy to see the pharmacist among them and watched as Paul said something to her that produced a smile before she climbed in. Paul was a gossip, the last person Dominic wanted around their new worker. He would make sure that ended fast, he thought as he shut the tailgate.

Gregoire waved to Dominic before driving into the vines. Paul followed and Dominic brought up the rear. When they reached the designated *terroir*, he shut off the motor and walked around to open the tailgate.

After the workers used the ladder to get down, he climbed up and opened the locker. "Before you follow the others, I'm handing out scissors, gloves and knee pads for all of you to use while you work here. For those of you who have done this before, you know the gloves help prevent stains, but it's your choice whether to wear them or not. I presume you've brought water bottles and sunscreen." Everyone nodded and waited their turn.

"At the end of the day, more trucks will be here to take you back to the tent area."

In a few minutes they were ready and followed Gregoire and Paul's groups, lining up and down the rows of grapes to get started. Dominic took a walk along another row, satisfied to see that the trailer had arrived for the collectors who gathered the picked grapes to transport to the winery.

When Paul had to leave to help some of the other workers, Dominic took advantage of the moment to catch Mademoiselle Fournier alone. She was kneeling on the pad and had started cutting grapes. He noticed her gloves stuck in one of the back pockets of her jeans.

"*Bonjour*, mademoiselle."

She looked up in surprise, giving him the full view of her light green eyes. The woman's beauty took his breath away.

"*Bonjour*, monsieur."

"You prefer not to use gloves?"

"Maybe I'll put them on later, but I need to practice without them first to get a feel for the work."

He was surprised as that's what he would have advised. Paul had obviously shown her what to do and already she'd put some grapes in the bucket provided.

"Did you apply sunscreen already?"

"I did at the last minute."

"That's good. The heat is already building. You don't want to get a sunburn before the end of your first day. You'll also likely find you need an over-the-counter painkiller to deal with aches and pains tonight."

An enticing smile broke out on her lovely face. "I brought some just in case. That's very kind of you to be concerned."

"*He*, Dominic."

"*Salut*, Paul." The other man had come back. Dominic still held her green gaze. "Just remember not to kill yourself off today. You'll need your strength for tomorrow."

She smiled. "I appreciate the warning. *Merci*, monsieur."

Dominic nodded to Paul, then walked toward the truck in the distance. On his way back to the office, he ate his snacks, but he'd need coffee. To his relief Theo had already made it for both of them.

No sooner had Dominic poured himself a cup and walked into his private office to get busy than Raoul arrived. All the family offices were in the same building.

"You're a sight for sore eyes, *mon vieux*. Come on in and shut the door."

"I was hoping you'd be here." He'd brought a cup of coffee with him and planted himself on a leather chair opposite Dominic's desk.

"Anything new at the conference in Saint Tropez?"

Raoul shook his head. "The Provencal vineyards seem to be doing marginally better, but it's going to take years before every vintner in France recoups losses from two years ago. *Dieu merci* for the personal investments you've helped me make."

"You're not worried about money, are you?"

"I might be."

"That sounded cryptic."

"Let's just say I'd like you to go over my accounts and let me know what I'm worth. I might need some of it before long."

Dominic sat forward. "I'll look into it before the day is out. But promise me you're not thinking of doing something drastic."

"Like what?"

"I don't know. Like leaving the way *I* did, maybe?"

He knew his cousin's marriage had been in shambles from the start, and that both Raoul and his wife carried a deep sorrow from losing their little girl, Celine, who had died at one month from a bad heart. Dominic wondered how much longer the two could keep up pretensions.

"My greatest regret is that I didn't go to Paris with you years ago. Let's face it, Dom. You were the only one in the family with the guts to get out before being swallowed alive."

"But I'm back now." For how long he didn't know. It depended on Nathalie Fournier, who'd swept into his life on Friday, bringing a beauty and charm that had put some kind of a spell on him. His desire to get to know her had stoked an unprecedented hunger in him, though his cousin didn't know that.

Raoul stared hard at him. "Yes, but you're still free to make your own decisions. Nobody owns you and your life is intact."

"No one owns you, Raoul."

"You're right. I take ownership for my guilt and mistakes with Sabine."

Dom let out a troubled sigh. "As you can see, the tentacles brought me back temporarily."

"The day you came home was my salvation."

"You're mine, Raoul. Whatever you're planning, don't leave."

"Not yet anyway. I need to know where I stand financially before I do anything."

"I'll get busy on it." Something serious was going on with Raoul.

"Thanks. Now enough about me. I hear Etienne is still sick."

"He's finally getting better. I'm filling in for him a while longer, but something odd has come up I want to talk to you about."

"Go ahead."

Dominic told him everything, but didn't reveal the strength of his attraction to the pharmacist. "Am I being paranoid that she's up to something questionable?"

Raoul studied him for a minute. "Being an undercover freelance reporter is a big stretch from being a pharmacist. But I'd trust your instincts as they're rarely wrong. If you feel something isn't right, then it isn't. What's your plan?"

"I'm going to get to know her."

"After a few days you'll know if she's out for a scoop on the business. It has happened before. Grand-père forced the perpetrators to pay stiff fines and do jail time."

"That's our grandfather." Dominic didn't want her to have to face that type of punishment for trespassing. If that was what she was doing.

Just then, Raoul received a text. After reading it, he looked up. "I've got to get over to my office."

"I'll call you tonight."

"What would I do without you in my corner?"

On that note, he dashed off.

Dominic sat back, pondering his cousin's counsel to follow his instincts about Miss

Fournier. He planned to find out what made her tick.

After pulling all the information on Raoul's investments, he did some figures and prepared a form to give his cousin. By afternoon he'd finished his work, so he drove his car back out to the *terroir*. Dominic made sure he'd shown up early enough to catch sight of the woman who was constantly on his mind.

Paul and Gregoire kept moving up and down the rows to help the workers. At 4:30 p.m. he saw her and several others leave the vineyard, though she walked down the road rather than climb into one of the trucks.

Dominic called to her as he pulled his car alongside her on the road. "Mademoiselle Fournier?"

She swung toward him, her eyes lighting up when she saw him behind the wheel. "*Bonsoir*, monsieur."

"Since I'm on my way back to the chateau, allow me to drive you to your mobile home."

"Oh—thank you very much." It surprised

him that without hesitation she climbed in the other side with her backpack.

He started driving at a slow pace. "How was your first day?"

A fetching smile broke out on her flushed face. "You don't want to hear about it."

Her comment made him laugh. "It had to be a change from preparing prescriptions for people."

"Working here with the vines is another existence. No matter how sore I am, it makes you part of this world of living greenery." She had a unique way of putting things that seemed to confirm his suspicions that she could be a writer. She darted him a smile. "How was *your* day?"

Was she trying to get information from him? "You'd be bored to tears." In truth he'd accomplished less than usual and it was all because of the beautiful woman sitting next to him.

"I'm sure that's not true. For my part, I already feel a camaraderie with some of the other workers. The Lopez family next to me is so cheerful."

Dominic remembered interviewing them after she'd left the tent. "It doesn't sound like you're ready to quit yet."

"Oh, no. I'm in for the count."

"Why?" More than ever he wanted an answer to that question.

"I learned as a child that way back when one of your ancestors was titled and given this land. Not very many people can claim a heritage like yours. It made fascinating reading."

All her answers sounded truthful. "Why fascinating?"

"When I was a little girl, I grew up on fairy tales. Your chateau is the embodiment of those painted on the covers of the books I loved. The thought of working in your vineyard sounded intriguing. Is it true your grandfather holds the title of Duc?"

"It's a defunct title." Maybe she was writing an historical account for a publisher and wanted information from the CEO himself. Did she hope for permission from Dominic?

"Even so, it adds a certain mystique from the past that makes you and your family seem out of the ordinary. When I was at the Guinguet, I noticed several paintings of the chateau and sculptured gardens hanging on the walls. It's very cool."

Minute by minute she was enamoring him. Eventually they reached the park. "Where is your mobile home?"

"It's the third one in the second row."

He kept driving and pulled up behind a blue car. Now that he knew where to find her, he didn't want to let her go. She had a vitality that intrigued him. Much as he wanted to take her to dinner this evening, he knew she was exhausted after her first day.

"Voilà, mademoiselle. Home in one piece."

"Bed is going to feel good tonight."

He could imagine. "I'll see you tomorrow."

"Thank you more than you know."

She got out of the car and he watched her until she waved to him and let herself inside the mobile home. When he was convinced she was safely inside, he backed up and left the park. Tomorrow he had plans for the two of them.

CHAPTER THREE

TUESDAY MORNING NATHALIE woke up at
5:00 a.m. with new aches and pains. Picking
grapes was a killer, but she was determined
to see this through. Whether he was Alain's
father or not, the hope of seeing Dominic
again was all she could think about. The
man had already captivated her. He had a
polish that attracted her to him like mad.

After showering, she hurriedly dressed and
tied her hair back, covering herself in sunscreen. After eating breakfast, she packed a
sandwich, fruit and water in her backpack,
where she'd left the knee pads and scissors.
Then she stole from the house.

Right now Alain was still sound asleep.
So was her mom, who wouldn't open the
pharmacy until eight. She'd hired Denis Vo-
lant, another pharmacist from Nice, to help

run things while she was undercover at the vineyard. Minerve, the woman who tended Alain, was scheduled to arrive at the house at 7:30 a.m.

Already the air was warm and once again it seemed that it would prove to be a hot day. Nathalie drove along the road to the mobile home and parked her car around the side. After freshening up inside, she left and started walking toward the workers' tent at the vineyard to wait for the truck.

But that meant Paul would be there. Having no desire to encourage him, she changed her mind. As she started out for the *terroir* on foot, she was surprised when a familiar sleek black Renault sedan drove past her.

She glanced at the driver. The sight of Dominic Fontesquieu caused her heart to leap. Everything about him spoke of sophistication and a privileged life most people would never know anything about. It was there in his manner and speech.

He pulled to the side ahead of her on the roadway and got out of the car. In jeans and a pale gray crew neck, his male charisma was devastating. Those black eyes played over her.

"You're still alive," he murmured in that deep voice she loved.

She smiled. "Barely."

"That's honest at least."

"You did warn me."

His hands went to his hips in a totally male stance. "Then I suggest you get in my car now to reserve your strength."

"That's very nice of you, but I don't want to put you out."

"Not at all. I can't allow word to get around that one of our new pickers has been worked to exhaustion after her first day."

She laughed gently. After hoping she'd see him today, she didn't dare let this precious opportunity get away. "You're a lifesaver. Thank you, monsieur."

"My name is Dominic." He opened the passenger door for her so she could get in carrying her backpack. He'd just thrown her a lifeline to get to know him better.

The interior smelled of the soap he used, teasing her senses. In a minute he'd climbed behind the wheel and they were off to the *terroir* in the distance. "I pass by here several times a day checking on the carriers. If ever you need a ride, just let me know."

Encouraged by the offer, she said, "I might take you up on that since by the end of the day I'm quite sure I won't have enough strength to climb in one of the trucks. You weren't kidding when you said I'd need painkiller."

"The pain will pass."

"I hope so. I've never appreciated the kind of hard work involved. While I was cutting grapes, I marveled to think of all the care needed to keep the vineyard healthy and thriving. No one should complain about the price of wine. Ninety-nine percent of the world has no clue what goes into making it."

He darted her an amused glance. "That's quite a testimonial. What's your favorite kind?"

"I don't have one. I dislike the taste of wine and much prefer to eat the grapes."

A burst of deep male laughter came out of him.

"I know that sounds crazy, especially when you work for a vineyard, but I just don't care for it, and I really despise the sour white wine they serve at the Guinguet."

"You mentioned that yesterday."

Did it bring back memories of being there with Antoinette?

"That's right. One of the workers suggested I go there to relax, so Friday evening I drove there and looked around before driving home. Monsieur Cortier saw me and asked if I'd like to try their famous sour wine." She shook her head. "It was awful. He said it comes from the Fontesquieu winery, but I can't imagine anyone wanting to drink it."

"I don't like it either."

"You're not offended by my frank speaking?"

"Not at all."

Too soon they'd arrived at the *terroir*. Afraid he would realize how much she was enjoying their conversation, she got out of the car. "You saved my life giving me this ride."

"It was my pleasure. I'd like to get to know you better—why don't I come by at noon to take you to the winery for lunch? Since you don't like wine, it ought to be an interesting experience for you to see how the other half lives."

His smile thrilled her. "You'd do that?"

"A man has to eat. I'd rather have company."

"So would I."

Dominic Fontesquieu had a sense of humor and was incredibly easy to talk to. When she'd been hired on here, she'd been intent on finding Alain's father. She'd never expected that she'd meet a man who swept her away with every look and smile. The fact that he could have been Antoinette's lover made this whole situation more complicated. "*A bientôt*, Dominic."

He leaned across the seat. "I'm sorry, I don't recall your name."

Her heart thumped. "It's Nathalie."

"*A bientôt*, Nathalie."

He'd just said he'd see her soon. Once again the sound of that low male voice wound its way to her insides.

A tremor of excitement raced through her as she shut the door and hurried toward the row where she'd been working. Without looking back, she could hear the engine as he drove away. Her hope to spend time with him was coming to fruition much sooner than she'd anticipated.

He'd said he wanted to get to know her better. He wasn't the only one. It shocked her how much she longed to be with him again. For someone of his status, there wasn't an atom of arrogance in him, which made him so appealing she couldn't get enough of him.

Before long the trucks came with the workers and she plunged into her day. But knowing Dominic would be picking her up at noon carried her through the rest of her morning. His irresistible charm had seeped its way beneath her skin and she found herself thinking constantly about him. That was a side effect she hadn't anticipated when she'd considered trying to look for Alain's father.

But therein lay a problem. She needed to learn a bit more about him before she revealed why she'd come to the vineyard in the first place. That meant she had to close off her personal feelings about him because this was all about Alain. She couldn't let it be about her desire for the man himself. She just couldn't!

"Did you know you're talking to yourself?"

She snipped another bunch of grapes in frustration before glancing at Paul. *"Bonjour."*

"How about going out with me after work tonight? I know you don't want a relationship, but can't we be friends at least?"

"Of course, but I'm afraid I have plans."

"Is there a night when you'll be free?"

Nathalie wasn't interested, but didn't want to be rude since he was one of the supervisors here. "Maybe Thursday evening right after work? Get a pizza? I saw a pizzeria near the Guinguet."

He nodded. "Thursday it is. I'll pick you up."

"No, no. I'll meet you there in my car."

She heard him sigh. "Have it your way."

"Thanks for understanding. *Ciao*, Paul."

When he moved on, she got back to work. As for Dominic, Nathalie realized she couldn't allow the situation about Alain to go on much longer before telling him why she'd come.

Nathalie kept checking her watch. When it was noon, she grabbed her backpack and hurried out to the road. Dominic sat in his car waiting for her. She couldn't believe how excited she was to see and talk to him.

He reached across the seat and opened the door for her. When she climbed in, he put her pack in the back, then flashed her a smile that melted her bones.

"You came!" The white crew neck shirt brought out his olive skin. He was such a striking man with that black hair and all-seeing black eyes, she could hardly breathe.

"As if I wouldn't," his voice grated and they took off down the road.

"I'm so lucky to be whisked away in the middle of the day."

"It's a treat for me too."

Something was going on here. She knew how she was feeling about him, about how she'd felt the moment she'd met him. It was like an explosion going off inside her. If she wasn't mistaken, he was just as attracted and couldn't stay away from her.

Was he the man Antoinette had met? Her conflict was growing. How ironic that Nathalie had hoped to find Alain's father, yet now that she thought Dominic could be the one, a part of her didn't want him to be the man her stepsister had loved.

Before long they approached a chateau that looked older and smaller than the main chateau. There were clusters of cars parked outside. Dominic drove around the back of it. "We'll eat lunch first, then I'll take you on a tour before you have to return to work."

After he'd helped her out of the car, Dominic took her inside a vaulted room with some interesting framed documents and pictures to do with wine. The place was filled with tourists seated at tables drinking wine and enjoying lunch.

Once he'd found them a table in the corner, he deserted her long enough to talk to the aproned man behind the ancient-looking bar. Armed with two bottles of Perrier water and two *croques monsieurs*, he returned.

She took a bite of the melted ham and cheese sandwich. "Mmm. I haven't had one of these in ages. It's delicious. Does every winery offer food like this?"

"Not many."

"The sales must skyrocket after someone has been here."

He finished his food. "That's the idea." His eyes gleamed as he looked at her. "I can get you coffee if you'd prefer it."

"Thank you, but water is much better while I'm working."

"I couldn't agree more. When you're ready, I'll show you around the winery."

"Let's go now. I'd love to see everything possible before I have to get back. I don't want Gregoire to think I'm taking advantage."

"We can't have that." That slow smile made her pulse race.

She held on to her half-full bottle of water and followed him through a door that led to the heart of the building. The huge vaulted rooms filled with machinery and barrels overwhelmed her. The place reminded her of a scientist's laboratory all devoted to producing sumptuous wines that kept the Fontesquieu Corporation one of the top winemakers in the world.

Dominic smiled at her while they walked from room to room. "You're not saying anything."

That was because his native intelligence pretty much staggered her. "I'm too busy marveling over this amazing world. I'm afraid I feel guilty that I don't like wine."

A chuckle escaped him. "Your liver is much healthier leaving it alone."

"I don't think I dare quote you," she quipped, loving this hour spent with him while he explained the winemaking process, overwhelming her with knowledge he'd been learning since birth. He knew so much about everything that it seemed he could go on forever, but it was past time to leave. "I should get back to work."

"I was afraid you'd say that," he whispered. "I'll explain to Gregoire it was my fault that you're late. Come this way."

Dominic led her to another exit not used by the public and they walked around the building to his car. As he cupped her elbow, his touch sent a dart of electricity through her body, making her come alive.

He helped her in before driving her back to the *terroir*. After he stopped, he said, "Since I don't want this day to end, why don't I pick you up after work?"

She sensed he wanted to be with her as much as she wanted to be with him. It was hard to believe this was really happening. "Only if you have time."

"I'll make it," he declared in a firm tone of voice that sent an unmistakable message of his desire to be with her.

"Thank you for lunch and the tour, Dominic. To be shown around by an expert has been a highlight for me I'll never forget." She meant what she'd said and knew she sounded breathless.

"That makes two of us."

He handed her the backpack before she got out of the car. Their hands touched, once again making her feel weak with longing. Nathalie walked to the row where she'd been snipping grapes. When she reached her spot, she finished the bottled water and got busy, counting the minutes until she could be with Dominic again.

When the heat reached its zenith, Nathalie checked her watch. It was four thirty. Quitting time. She gathered up her things, so eager to see Dominic, it was ridiculous. But after reaching the road, there was no sign of his car. Undoubtedly something had held him up because she knew he'd had every intention of coming for her.

Disappointed, she avoided the trucks and started to walk toward the mobile home, anxious to get out of the hot sun. Three-quarters of the way back, she saw the black Renault coming toward her. It shouldn't thrill her to see him, but it did. She was in so much trouble. When she'd followed through on her plan, she hadn't considered being enthralled by the man she'd been searching for.

He stopped and got out. "I'm sorry to be late, but it couldn't be helped."

"Please don't apologize. I know you're a busy man."

In seconds he'd opened the passenger door. This time their arms brushed as she climbed inside, making her acutely aware of him. The AC felt wonderful and she was relieved she didn't have to walk. He made a U-turn and drove them back toward the mobile park.

He pulled up behind her blue Peugeot. "Why don't you go in and freshen up, then we'll drive somewhere for a bite to eat before I bring you back here. Lunch didn't fill me and I'm starving."

"I'm hungry too. Thanks. I'll be out soon."

His invitation opened up a whole evening where she could learn more about his personal life. Totally intoxicated by him, Nathalie slid out of the car and unlocked the door of the mobile home. She hurried inside and took a quick shower. After putting on jeans and a blouse, she brushed her hair.

Her body trembled on the way out to his car because her feelings for him were growing to the point he was all she could think about. She hurried back to the car and got in. "Where are we going?"

"I've ordered us some takeout so you can stay in the car and rest while we eat."

A soft laugh escaped her lips. "Only someone who has picked grapes before would understand how I feel."

He started the car and drove them out to the main road into Vence. "It was my first job. I think I was about four when my *papa* walked me and my five-year-old brother, Etienne, to the vineyard and showed us what to do."

She turned to him. "Did you live near this one when you were little?"

In the next breath, he said, "Are you going to tell me that after Paul plied you with sour wine, he didn't tell you who I am?"

Oh, boy. She'd walked right into that one. "No. I was only trying to be discreet. Paul *did* say you were a Fontesquieu, but the last thing I've wanted to do is presume anything and he didn't go into detail."

Dominic didn't respond. Within seconds he turned a corner and pulled up in front of a café. "I'll be right out. After I get back, you can tell me why you really came to the vineyard for work you don't need."

She groaned inwardly. Nathalie wasn't

wrong about his being strongly attracted to
her, but it was clear he hadn't believed her
reason for being here.

He soon returned with their food and
headed toward the Fontesquieu estate once
more. After he pulled to a stop and shut off
the engine, he handed her cannelloni, salad
and an espresso.

"Thank you, Dominic. This smells and
looks delicious." But her heart was pounding so hard, she feared he could hear it.

He tucked into his meal before turning to
her. "Now, how about telling me what newspaper or wine magazine you're working for
undercover?"

Her heart plummeted. "Is that why you
showed me around the winery?"

"I took you there because I wanted to be
with you, and because I was hungry. But
in case you were after a story, I thought I'd
show you the inner workings, something not
everyone is allowed to see. If you've been
hired by a newspaper to find out how the

migrant workers are treated at the vineyard, I wanted to give you a favorable impression."

She ate her food, trying to find the right words. Obviously their family had been bothered by infiltrators before. Nathalie couldn't blame him for being suspicious since she didn't meet the profile of the normal picker.

"I'm not a spy, Dominic. Your assumptions are understandable, but they would be wrong about me," she said in a quiet voice. "Is it impossible for you to imagine that I simply want to work here for a few weeks to enjoy a new experience?"

His black eyes bored into hers, reminding her of Alain. "Yes. Our background check proves you're a full-time pharmacist. If you're truly not here undercover, why don't you tell me the truth about why you chose to work at this specific vineyard for a few weeks?"

She finished her espresso. "This is embarrassing."

"I'm listening." He'd never taken his eyes off her.

"Three months ago I broke up with a pharmaceutical distributor. We met in graduate school in Nice several years ago and continued to see each other off and on. After Christmas I thought maybe he could be the one. But in time I realized we were wrong for each other." Guy's reaction to her being unable to have children had worried her that another man would probably feel the same way. She couldn't help wondering if the man sitting next to her would reject her for the same reason. "Since I'd already arranged my vacation time for a trip we obviously did not end up taking, I decided to do something different that would bring me a little money, not cost me."

"Vintners are noted for paying lower wages," he murmured.

"Nevertheless, I need to save all I can for the future." Now came the lie. "After passing your vineyard, I saw that you were hiring workers for the three-week harvest and thought it would be a fascinating way for me to spend my vacation from the pharmacy.

"I also believed that working with the soil would be so different, it would be cathartic for me. There's nothing like a new challenge." Considering she was doing this for Alain's sake, she hoped lightning wouldn't strike her. "But you would have every right to tell me to walk away now."

"Is that what I'm doing?" he asked in a silky tone.

"No. I'm offering to go." She didn't have enough proof he could be Alain's father to confront him. "If you'll wait long enough for me to get my backpack, I'll return the equipment handed to me. The man running the mobile home park will be glad if I give up mine since there's always a demand for one." She started to get out.

"Wait—" he said, reaching for her arm. She felt his touch to her toes. "You're doing an excellent job, according to Gregoire's nightly reports. Forgive me for jumping to the wrong conclusion about you. It's just that there's nothing my grandfather dislikes more than someone who trespasses on the property for ulterior motives."

"Of course, and you had every right to be suspicious of me when it's clear I'm not desperate for a job."

I'm only desperate for answers.

"That's very generous of you," he murmured. "Maybe you won't believe me, but I'm sorry if I've offended you. Let's hope working with the vines might work its magic for you, even if you dislike the taste of wine." The sudden smile he flashed was enough to reduce her to jelly. "You're not fired, Nathalie."

His ability to admit he'd been wrong made her admire him more than he'd ever know, but she was also filled with raw guilt because she hadn't told him the real reason she'd come. All she needed was a little more information.

"Thank you for a second chance, and for buying me dinner."

"To prove I'm telling you the truth, I'd like

to take you on a walk through the vineyard tomorrow evening after you've eaten. You mentioned you'd like to see more of it while we were at the winery. Will your aching joints be able to handle it?"

She turned to him. "There's nothing I'd love more," she whispered.

"Jusqu'à demain soir," he whispered back.

Arriving back home, she climbed out of his car and rushed inside the mobile home, where he couldn't see her breakdown. Nathalie had to face the truth. It had been only a few days, but she'd already fallen hard for him. Love at first sight was no joke. Nothing like this had ever happened to her before.

It wasn't just his dashing dark looks or the background he'd come from. He was a man of extraordinary substance. There was a kind of nobility about him. That's what made it so difficult for her to understand his behavior if he'd had an affair with Antoinette.

If he was the one who'd fathered her child,

how could he have disappeared on her step-sister with no explanation? Nathalie needed to learn the truth about him soon and not get carried away by her growing feelings for him.

He'd shaken her with his ability to see inside her and question her motives. She should have told him the truth, but had held back because of too little proof. One thing she knew by now. You didn't play games with a man like him.

Dominic's mind reeled as he drove home.

He'd wanted to believe Nathalie's explanation even though he felt she was still hiding something from him. Why it bothered him so much was a mystery to him. A virtual stranger couldn't possibly be this important to him no matter how beautiful or intriguing.

But the closer he got to the chateau, he knew that wasn't true. He'd been intimate with some attractive women over the years, yet nothing remotely like this had ever happened to him before.

Even if Nathalie was to disappear suddenly and he never saw her again, the fact that he could be swept away by her this fast had changed him in a fundamental way. Nathalie had lit a fire that wasn't going to go out.

It seemed there *was* a woman out there for him, one he wanted to get to know and would do whatever it took to do so. She was an original with a verve and freshness that was a constant delight to him. Her thoughts about everything fascinated him. If he believed in witches, he'd think she'd put him under a magical spell.

Dominic didn't know he could feel this way about a woman. Meeting her had revealed the real reason why he'd reached the age of twenty-nine and still hadn't married. Was it possible he'd unknowingly been waiting for her to come into his life?

He entered his apartment a different man. Needing more coffee, he went in the kitchen to fix it, then called his cousin and gave him the figures he wanted. Silence followed. "Raoul? Why aren't you saying anything?"

"I'm surprised that much money has accrued. It's all because of your expertise. But I'm afraid I may need more than that."

He took a deep breath. "Talk to me."

"When I got home from Saint Tropez Monday night, I told Sabine I was filing for divorce."

Dominic let out a sound, overjoyed for him. "That's the best news I've ever heard."

"Except that you don't know the bottom line."

He frowned. "What do you mean?"

"I can't go into it now. Can you meet me at our usual place Thursday evening to talk?"

"Of course."

"Suffice it to say all hell has broken loose. The family has already heard about it, and it's getting ugly."

"I've got your back all the way. You know what I mean."

"I do. Before we hang up, tell me about you."

"I wish I knew."

"Why do I have a feeling this is about Mademoiselle Fournier?"

He paced. "I was with her this morning, at lunch and after work."

"All in one day? You've got to be kidding me!"

"I know I sound like I've lost my mind. She's not who I thought she was, but I still don't know why she came here."

"And I can tell you're not going to give up until you get answers. I take it she's a knockout."

"You have no idea. I didn't know I could have feelings this fast for another woman."

"That's how it happened with me. One evening while I was checking on the inventory at the Guinguet I met Toinette. As you know, my world changed that night when I called and told you about her. But circumstances forced me to break off with her in order to marry Sabine. I've never been the same since. Thank heaven you're back home and not in Paris because I need to reveal a truth you don't know about yet. I'll tell you on Thursday. For now, I've got to go."

Raoul rang off before a puzzled Dominic could say goodbye. No matter how bad it got, he was thrilled Raoul had decided to get out of his marriage. He'd do whatever he could to help his cousin.

As for his own situation, before any more time passed, Dominic needed to talk to Corinne. He didn't want to put this off any longer. It wasn't fair to her to let her go on expecting an imminent marriage proposal. She was attractive. Dominic knew she'd meet another man, hopefully one who would love her for who she was, whether she came from money or not. She deserved to find true happiness. So did he.

Once he told her the truth and ended any thoughts her parents had put in her mind about marrying him, her pride might be hurt, but it was the only way to handle what their two families had tried to set up.

He had his own life to live. And now that he'd met Nathalie Fournier, he couldn't imagine her not being in his life.

CHAPTER FOUR

"MAMAN?"

Wednesday evening had come. Dominic would be arriving shortly to show her around the vineyard. It was a beautiful evening and she was going crazy waiting for him so had called her mother to check in.

"Yes. What is it, darling?"

Nathalie had left work to eat dinner and was freshening up in the mobile home. She'd brushed her hair, leaving it loose, and wore a fresh pair of jeans and a yellow pullover. "I'll be home a little later than usual and don't want you to worry."

"That's all I've done since our talk. I don't think it's wise to keep this up. Either walk away now, or tell Dominic Fontesquieu why you're there."

"I will. I just need a little more information

and to think everything through. If worse comes to worst and he demands an explanation, I'll tell him the truth. Depending on the outcome, I'll bring him to the house so he can see Alain for himself."

Her mother's sigh was telling. "You could be wrong and it could cause trouble."

"It won't come to that, Maman. When I get home, we'll talk."

After they hung up, her mother's concern ate away at her. Was Nathalie wrong about Dominic having been Antoinette's lover? Of course, the only way to find out was to ask him and hope he'd be honest with her.

But to approach him about such a sensitive matter was daunting. "Did you have a brief affair with a woman you met at the Guinguet during the harvest two and half years ago? If so, then I believe you could be the father of my deceased stepsister's son."

Deep in thought, she was startled by noise outside. He was here. A burst of adrenaline shot through her. She reached for her purse and hurried out the door. Dominic had parked his car behind hers and Nathalie climbed in the passenger side before he could get out.

"Hi," she said, knowing that once again she was out of breath. It happened every time she saw him. He smelled so good and had dressed in a blue sport shirt and khaki trousers. There could be no other man like him in existence.

His black eyes ranged over her, taking in every inch. "You look too beautiful for a woman who's been picking grapes all day."

"That isn't true, but I like hearing it."

"If you'd glance in a mirror, it would remove all doubt."

His words brought heat flooding to her cheeks. "Where are we going to go?"

"I thought we'd take a walk in one of the *terroirs* at the upper elevation. It overlooks the land down to the sea for a spectacular view."

The male sight before her eyes was so spectacular, she was at a loss for words.

He backed around and drove down the road past the place where she picked grapes. When they came to a crossroads, he turned right and followed another road. It paralleled more rows of healthy vines for a long time, then rose until he pulled over to the side and parked.

"The grapes have all been picked here," she observed.

"That's right. They've turned a few days sooner because of the elevation. The *terroir* you're working on is one of the last that has to be denuded."

She shook her head. "There's so much to learn. Tonight the vines seem to be lined up like soldiers to the horizon. It's an amazing sight. If I were an artist, I'd like to paint the vineyard the way it looks right now. I love it."

"I love your descriptions of everything." The tone in his deep voice filled her with warmth. "This is my favorite spot in the whole vineyard."

After getting out of the car, she let out a soft cry. "I can see why, Dominic. This landscape is like a little part of heaven."

He grasped her hand as if claiming her. They started walking between two rows of vines. A gentle breeze bathed their bodies. "You know what Louis Pasteur once said. A bottle of wine contains more philosophy than all the books in the world."

"Fontesquieu wine," she corrected him. He squeezed her hand a little harder. "I feel horribly guilty that I don't like the taste of wine."

"But you like the grapes." He gave her a meaningful look. "All is forgiven because you appreciate the vineyard housing the limestone and shale soil that feeds the roots."

A gentle laugh escaped. "Thank you for trying to make me feel better."

"You mean I didn't succeed?" he teased.

"You *know* you did." He had a captivating way about him.

They kept walking beneath a sky full of

stars. As their bodies brushed against each other, she'd never known such rapture in her life. At the end of the row, he moved behind her and put his hands on her shoulders.

"Did you know your hair is the color of starlight?"

She could feel his breath on her temple. "Dominic—" His name came out sounding ragged.

A kiss against her neck opened the portals, releasing her longing for him. She turned in his arms and began to kiss his jaw, relishing the feel of his hard, male body. Their mouths slowly came together, seeking and finding what she'd wanted from the moment she'd sat across from him. This was ecstasy. Never in her life had she known this kind of passion.

When he finally relinquished her mouth with reluctance, he said, "Don't you know how dangerous it was to come out here with me tonight?"

His question penetrated deep inside to that spot reminding her they wouldn't be together like this if she weren't trying to find out if he'd been Antoinette's lover. For a little while tonight she'd forgotten.

Shocked by how carried away she'd been, she looked up at him. "Thank you for reminding me. Maybe we'd better go back." Nathalie eased out of his arms and started walking fast, reaching the car first.

He didn't try to catch up with her. While she was a trembling mass of need, Dominic seemed in perfect control driving them down to the mobile home park. He stopped behind her car and turned to her.

"I won't be able to see you tomorrow, but I'd like to see you after work Friday evening if you're free. We'll go to dinner."

Friday evening… That would have to be the night she asked him about Antoinette. "I'll make sure I am." She got out of the car. "I won't ever forget tonight's experience."

With her heart palpitating out of her chest, she rushed inside. The kiss they'd shared had turned her world upside down. To love a man like him, and have to tell him she couldn't have his baby...

After work on Thursday, Nathalie drove to the pizzeria in town and met Paul outside the entrance. They made their way inside and had to wait before being shown a table with menus propped on the red-and-white-checked cloth. She could tell it was a popular place, especially at dinnertime.

After studying the menu, Paul flicked Nathalie a glance. "How do you like your pizza?"

"A little bit of everything except for anchovies."

"Sounds good to me. Anything else?"

"Coffee."

A waitress came over for their order and hurried off.

Nathalie eyed Paul. "Wouldn't it be nice if the Fontesquieu family hired a food catering service that pulled into the vineyard every noon and evening? Think how happy it would make all the workers!"

He smiled. "That's a thought I'll pass on to Gregoire." But not to Dominic or Etienne, either of whom could make it happen.

"I saw clouds gathering this afternoon."

"It'll rain tomorrow."

"I can feel the extra humidity. It ought to make grape picking more interesting."

He grinned. "You mean messy, dirty and wet."

"I guess I'm going to find out."

"Want to go to a film after we eat?"

She shook her head. "I have to get back to the pharmacy where I work and do inventory. That's why I brought my car."

"You're a pharmacist?" Surprise was written all over him.

"By profession."

"But I thought you were on vacation." He looked stunned. "You have to go tonight?"

She nodded. "They need help so I promised to come in."

"Even when you've got a full day's work tomorrow?"

"I can't turn down a promise."

"You're one amazing woman."

Thankfully their food arrived at that moment.

"This pizza is good."

"It's all right," he muttered. "I'd rather we went out for a real dinner."

"Honestly, I'm too exhausted working seven days a week to do anything but fall asleep watching TV. Monsieur Fontesquieu warned me to take it easy so I don't burn out and collapse. Actually, he saw me walking and gave me a lift home the other day. It was very kind of him. If he has a wife who knows about it, I hope she'll understand he was only helping a lowly, exhausted grape picker make her way along the road."

Paul shook his head. "He's never been married."

The unexpected news filled her with joy for several reasons. "I see."

"Not yet, at least. According to Gregoire, who's on close terms with Etienne, Dominic Fontesquieu is on the verge of getting married to a woman with the kind of money most people only dream about."

After hearing he wasn't married, the revelation of impending marriage to a wealthy woman came as a shock. If that was true, how could he have kissed Nathalie like he did last night? Or made plans to be with her tomorrow evening?

Distressed, she wiped the corner of her mouth with a napkin. "Paul, I'm afraid I have to leave." Nathalie pulled some euros out of her purse and put them on the table before standing up. "Stay and finish the pizza."

"Don't forget to wear extra rain gear in the morning."

"I will. See you in the morning. *Merci* for the friendly chat."

Nathalie was tormented as she sped home. After the kiss they'd shared, she didn't know what to think about Dominic. At least he didn't have a wife or children to consider if he were to learn he'd fathered Antoinette's baby. But if he were getting married soon, he shouldn't have been with Nathalie. Following that thought, the news that he had a son could turn his world upside down.

What was she doing? This couldn't go on any longer.

On Thursday, Dominic had been summoned to the salon of his parents' apartment at the chateau. He knew why.

His father, clearly recovered from his pneumonia, sat on one of the damask couches with his mother, whose stylish black hair showed a few streaks of silver. Dominic's older sister, Quinette, and her husband, Philippe, both serving on the board, had settled on the love seat. Etienne wasn't there because he hadn't shaken his flu completely.

He kissed his parents and sister and nodded to his brother-in-law, but he didn't sit down. "I came as soon as I could. It's obvious you've heard news before I could tell you myself."

"Corinne's mother called me this afternoon to tell me you won't be seeing her anymore."

"That's right, Maman. We've been thrown together at various family parties you arranged, but I never was *seeing* her."

"I simply don't believe it." Her voice shook. "She sounded hysterical. We've all been planning on your marriage."

"I can't help that. I'm not in love with Corinne, and she doesn't want to be married to a man who can't give her the kind of love she needs."

She turned to his father. "Talk to him, Gaston."

"I tried talking to him when he left home at eighteen. My foolish son has cavorted with Parisian women with no class for too long. His judgment disgusts me."

His chilling pronouncement couldn't disturb Dominic. His father was lamenting all the money Corinne would have brought to the marriage. "I'm aware of that, Papa, but I have to please myself."

His mother's dark eyes filled with tears. "What's wrong with you, Dominic?"

"Maman," his sister remarked. Having been stuck in a bad marriage, she'd begun to see the light and had taken his side.

He smiled at Quinette before he said, "If I ever find the right woman, you'll be the first to know, *ma mere*. In the meantime, if you'll excuse me, I have plans. *Bonne nuit*."

Now that his parents had let him know they were devastated, he left to meet Raoul at Chez Gaspard, a café on the outskirts of Vence where they could enjoy privacy.

They met there when they needed to talk away from the estate. Tonight there were two households in chaos at the chateau.

Raoul was already waiting for him when he entered and walked to the back table in the corner. The waiter brought coffee Raoul had already ordered for them. Once he'd left, Dominic handed Raoul the financial report.

"Thanks for this." He lifted his dark head and sat forward. "I promised you some new information. As you know, I'd been dating

Sabine and made the mistake of sleeping with her once, a mistake I regretted because as time went on I knew my feelings for a permanent relationship with her weren't there. I had to tell her the truth even though it hurt her and I broke it off with her.

"Right after that I happened to meet Toinette Gilbert and found myself in love for the first time in my life. She'd become my heart's desire. We saw each other for a month and I wanted to marry her.

"But out of the blue I got a phone call from Sabine. She told me she was expecting our baby and we had to get married immediately. Her doctor verified it with me.

"I was horrified. Of course, I had to tell Toinette the truth, the most painful thing I'd ever had to do in my life. She said goodbye to me and refused all my phone calls. I never saw her after that. My world had crashed around me."

Dominic could attest to that fact. "You did the honorable thing, Raoul. When I heard you two were expecting, I knew that was the only reason you would have married her, especially after telling me you were in love with Toinette. But what is it I still don't know?"

"I'm getting to that. Only the birth of little Celine helped me to go on. I loved our daughter and was devastated after she died. While I was at the hospital, I talked to the doctor and asked if her heart was the reason why she'd been born a month early. The doctor told me no. Celine had been a full-term baby."

A gasp came out of Dominic. "So the baby wasn't yours."

Raoul stared straight at him. "No. If I hadn't asked the doctor that question, Sabine would have kept that a secret for the rest of our lives. After coming home from Saint Tropez the other night, I decided it was time to tell her I was divorcing her, and I confronted her about the baby that wasn't mine."

"How did that go?"

"She admitted it. Her explanation was that

she'd always wanted me, but turned to another man because I'd never proposed."

"*Incroyable.* Did the other man ever know?"

"No," he said in a solemn voice.

"So you've been living with the pain of that lie ever since the funeral."

His cousin nodded. "Because you were in Paris, I didn't want to burden you. Instead I got some professional advice and was warned to put off a divorce until Sabine had recovered enough from Celine's death to deal with it."

A groan came out of Dominic. "How bad are things at this point?"

"Bad. I've been served papers from Sabine's attorney and have been talking with our attorney, Horace Millet."

"He's the best. What is she demanding?"

"Fifty million dollars in damages for lack of affection since she knew from the start I hadn't been in love with her. That was her excuse for being with another man while she waited for a proposal from me. She claimed she'd wanted marriage to me all her adult life." He sat back in the chair. "Well, she got it."

Dominic looked across at him. "You could countersue because of her lie."

"I could, but we've both been suffering over Celine's death. There's been too much grief as it is. I just want this period of my life over. Horace has drawn up papers declaring a legal separation. Since her attorney has indicated that Sabine is refusing to move out of the chateau until the divorce is final, I'm moving out. I've liquidated a few assets to keep functioning before Papa freezes my accounts. Both sets of parents are refusing to accept the divorce and are fighting it."

"Of course they are." And Raoul was too full of integrity to expose Sabine's lie to the family.

"For now I'm planning to live at the Aurora Hotel in Vence until this is over. I'm checking in there after I leave you."

"No, you're not. You're staying with me. I have two extra bedrooms. Both families are trying to take everything away from you.

That means I'm not letting you spend money on a hotel. You need to be close to the office."

"I can't do that to you."

"Raoul, if I were in your shoes, I know you'd tell me to move in with you, so let's not waste any more time talking about it. Come on. Follow me back to the chateau and let's get you moved in. While we do that, I'll fill you in on what's happening with me. It'll be fun. I've got more space in the apartment than I know what to do with."

"Dom—"

"We share a special bond, right?"

"Oui," his voice grated.

Dominic put some Euros on the table and they left for the chateau. Under the circumstances, he couldn't be happier to have his best friend close.

Within the hour, they'd set Raoul up in one of the bedrooms. His cousin eyed him as they both went to the kitchen for more coffee. "The family will have a collective heart attack when they find out the two bad boys have joined forces, but I could not care less. Have you ended it with Corinne yet?"

"I took care of that last night. When you texted me a little while ago, I was on my way to the parents to be castigated."

"How did that go?"

"According to Maman, Corinne's mother is in hysterics. I know I hurt Corinne for expectations never met, but there were no outward histrionics."

His cousin's dark brow lifted. "Let's change the subject. What's going on with Mademoiselle Fournier?"

"I haven't fired her yet if that tells you anything." Dominic was still shaken by the taste and feel of Nathalie, who'd welcomed his kiss last night with the same urgency he'd been feeling from the beginning.

"Do you still suspect her of something?"

"I don't know," he ground out. "Maybe I'm wrong and she's exactly who she says she is. After hearing about Sabine's lie of omission, I pray to God Nathalie has told me her whole truth by now."

His cousin eyed him with concern. "You sound like a man in love."

Dominic's head reared. "It may have finally happened, Raoul." But he would be in pain until he knew all of her and her heart.

"Does she feel the same way?"

"She hasn't said the words yet, but I know it in my gut." The way she'd kissed him had been proof of that.

Rain fell on Friday. Nathalie's work was wet and messy. She needed to shower and wash her hair after finishing work, as Dominic would be coming by to take her out for the evening.

Learning that he planned to be married soon had shaken her. If he were Alain's father and wanted a relationship with his boy, then how would Nathalie handle it? She was Alain's aunt and they would be sharing him. How was she going to shut off her feelings?

This evening she put on a pale blue short-sleeved blouse and a white skirt with a small blue print. She hadn't worn anything dressy around him. Her hair had natural curl. She brushed it until it swished against her shoulders from a side part, then she put on her leather sandals. Nathalie wore no makeup other than lipstick.

When he knocked on the door, she opened it and sucked in her breath. He stood there wearing a silky black shirt and gray trousers. No man had ever looked so devastatingly gorgeous to her. "Dominic—"

Tonight was her chance to ask him questions about Antoinette. She'd started down this path for Alain's sake and needed to see it through. "Thanks for being on time. I'm hungry again."

He chuckled and backed around. "And here I thought I'd have to wait. You're a constant surprise."

"So are you."

Dominic darted her an amused glance

with those gleaming black eyes before they got in the car and headed for Vence. He drove through the town and up into the hills. They wound around to a restaurant with date palms and cypress trees overlooking the breathtaking landscape.

He escorted her inside and they were shown to a table out on the veranda with a sweeping view. The waiter handed them menus.

"Everything's good here."

Nathalie looked over the options. "What's your favorite?"

"Suprême de veau rôti, crème provençale."

"That sounds delicious." She loved veal. "I'll try it."

The waiter came back with coffee and a wine list.

Dominic's gaze held hers as he told the waiter, "We'll pass on the wine." After giving him their order, the waiter walked off.

"I would imagine wine from the Fontesquieu vineyards makes up a good portion of every restaurant's list in Provence and elsewhere."

"My cousin Raoul could tell you all about it. He's in charge of marketing and sales."

"That has to be an enormous responsibility."

"But nothing like the responsibility you have as a pharmacist. When you make a mistake, it could be life threatening."

She nodded. "That's true."

"What made you choose that for your career?"

Now would be the perfect time to tell him about the family Alain had been born into.

"My parents were both pharmacists. That's how they met and got married. I was born soon after their marriage, then my *papa* died. I never knew him, only my stepfather, also a druggist who was a widower with a daughter. He married my mother. I grew up wanting to be a pharmacist too. After I graduated, they took me on at the pharmacy they owned."

"Sounds like my family."

"In a way." Their eyes held. "My step-father ran everything until he died several years ago."

"I'm sorry."

"So am I," she whispered. "Since then my mother has hired another pharmacist to help us."

"Do you live with your mother?"

"Yes." And one precious boy.

Their dinner came, interrupting their conversation. She started eating. "This veal is superb. I'm glad you suggested it."

"It never disappoints. Tell me, are you an only child?"

Her heart thudded. Stick to the truth as much as you dare. "No. I just had my step-sister, but she died sixteen months ago of an infection."

"Your family has known a lot of grief," he commiserated. "My parents lost a daughter right after she was born."

"They must have suffered."

"So have you after breaking up with the man you thought to marry."

She sipped her coffee. Since meeting Dominic, she hadn't given Guy a thought. "That has turned out to be a good thing. I can't imagine anything worse than getting married, only to discover you made a mistake. To settle when you already have questions about that person makes no sense to me."

"I couldn't agree more," he said with almost savage conviction. It sent a shiver down her spine.

Taking her courage in her hands, Nathalie said, "Rumor has it you will be getting married soon." She had to find out.

"Paul needs to be careful what he passes on, though it's not his fault what he hears. Marriage was never on my agenda. Otherwise I wouldn't have asked you to come to dinner with me this evening."

Heaven forgive her, but that news meant more to her than he would ever know. If she dared tell him about Alain, and he agreed to take a DNA test to prove paternity, he could be with his son without the complications of a new wife. But only if that was what Dominic wanted more than anything in his life. Alain deserved a father who would cherish him.

Knowing he wasn't getting married prompted her next question. "Why *did* you invite me out this evening, Dominic?"

His eyes narrowed on her mouth, making her whole body go limp. "You can ask me that after our walk in the vineyard?" She averted her eyes. "Because I wanted to." Somehow she felt he'd spoken the truth just now. "Why did you accept, Nathalie?"

Her heart thundered in her chest. "If I tell you the real reason, will you believe me?" They were both circling each other.

"I deserved that."

She was able to tell him one honest truth, though she was riddled with guilt. "Because *I* wanted to be with you too."

Dominic's chest rose and fell visibly, communicating an emotion that appeared to match hers. There was a growing sensual tension between them that couldn't be denied, haunting her more and more.

The waiter came over to suggest dessert. She declined. So did Dominic, who asked for the check. When it was paid, they left and went out to his car.

Nathalie looked up at the sky. "It's still overcast, but I don't think it will rain again tomorrow."

"It won't," he assured her and helped her into the car before walking around.

Once he was behind the wheel, she sent him a covert glance. "If you ever decide to give up being a vintner, you'll make a better weatherman than any meteorologist."

"I wouldn't want the job. They make too many mistakes. Technically I'm no longer a vintner. Not since I left for Paris eleven years ago and went into investment banking."

Eleven years? She blinked. When had there been time for him to meet Antoinette? Had she been wrong about him this whole time? "So you weren't born with grape juice running in your veins?" she teased.

He chuckled. "Maybe, but I was much

more interested in what made the world go round. Big business intrigued me."

Nathalie knew there was much more he hadn't told her, but this was a beginning. Before the night was out she might even learn enough to broach the subject of Alain.

CHAPTER FIVE

TWILIGHT HAD FALLEN over the town, giving it a magical look. Nathalie felt like they were the only two people who existed. Instead of driving her straight back to the mobile home, Dominic took her on a long drive around the other side of the vineyard, letting her see the vast property.

"The air smells so sweet, I feel like I'm in a dream. There's a peace here in the vineyard impossible to describe, yet it's alive. Glorious! I read an article on the Fontesquieu website that said there is something special about the manner in which vines in France attach themselves to the landscape. The author suggested that France is where the vines are *supposed* to be."

Dominic nodded. "My family believes as much."

"So do I."

He glanced at her. "When I took you to the winery, I wondered if you'd seen the plaque on the wall right by us."

"I did. It said, 'God planted the best vines on earth here in Provence.' I loved it." She drew in a deep breath. "Seeing all this with you, I believe it."

If the man sitting next to her had been Antoinette's heart's desire, it was understandable that she'd succumbed to him. But more and more Nathalie was beginning to feel that he wasn't Alain's father, and she didn't want this evening to end.

Maybe he was reading her thoughts because he said, "Do you mind if we make a detour to Saint Jeannet before I take you back home? My brother asked me to check on a special shipment of red wine my grandfather has been waiting for, and until Etienne gets better I'm trying to help him. It'll only be ten minutes out of our way."

The question filled her with exhilaration. This would give her more time to be with him. "Tell me about the shipment of red wine, Dominic. I thought you only produced rosé wine."

"We produce everything."

"Even sour wine."

He smiled. "That too."

"Will you tell me what you know about the emperor Charlemagne? I hear there's a story to do with him and red wine."

Dominic chuckled. "One of those stories is purported to have to do with his fourth or fifth wife. She was a beautiful German princess with many gifts and he adored her. When she died, he never remarried. But getting to the point, being a tall proud man with a prominent white beard, he wanted to look his best for her when they were married. Yet there was one problem."

Everything the brilliant man sitting next to her said or did enamored her. "What was that?"

"According to history, he was a big meat eater and red wine drinker. But she didn't like the red stains on his beard."

Nathalie studied the red stains on her own fingers and could well understand.

"Word has it that she demanded he drink only white wine. From then on only white grapes were commanded to be planted on a certain section of the hill. That's when Corton-Charlemagne in Burgundy was born and still continues."

"I had no idea. How fascinating."

"Except that it's partly myth. Other sources say it was Charlemagne's mother who didn't like her royal son looking terrible with those dreadful red stains."

She laughed. "That sounds more realistic."

"Are you ready for this? Some sources say he didn't have a beard. According to scholars, it was customary in the Middle Ages for artists to put facial hair on the rulers, symbolic of their virility."

"Oh, dear—don't tell me that and ruin this picture I have of Charlemagne with his *barbe fleurie*."

It was Dominic's turn to laugh that deep

laugh she loved. "Too much authentic research destroys most of our beliefs."

"You're right. It's much more fun to enjoy our own version of life. Since I'm with an expert and we're talking about red wine, please explain about red grapes having many secrets. I cherish the memory of you taking me on a tour of the winery."

His hand reached over to clasp hers, sending waves of longing through her body. Both their emotions were spilling over. "To keep it simple, all grape juice is white. Only the red skins contain a dark pigment. If the juice is separated from the skins shortly after being crushed, it remains white."

"I see."

"If the juice is left in contact with the red skins during fermentation, it becomes that delightful pink color. Left longer, it becomes red wine."

"I'm embarrassed to know so little about it."

He turned to her. "That's because you're not a wine drinker. Those who are show surprise to learn that eighty-eight percent of the wine produced in Provence is rosé. It has a delicious fruity flavor. Some people refer to it as summer water."

Another chuckle came out of her.

"Other drinkers prefer white wine, which is sweeter. Red wine is heavier. But as I explained, our winery produces everything."

During their conversation, she hadn't realized they'd reached the town of Saint Jeannet. He pulled up to a big warehouse before letting her go. He flicked his gaze to her. "I'll only be a minute."

The whole time they'd been talking, she realized she hadn't asked him any personal questions. But after hearing he'd been away from Vence for so many years, she was beginning to think he couldn't have been Antoinette's lover.

It was a lovely night to be out, and being with him was so stimulating to her, there weren't enough hours with him to satisfy everything she was desperate to know. Her whole body tingled from his touch.

He'd returned to the car while she'd been deep in thought. "Let's go."

"Was the shipment there?"

"Not yet. I need to inform Etienne." He pulled out his phone to text him, then started the car and they left for Vence.

"Will your grandfather be upset?"

"I'm afraid he was born in that condition, but he'll live to see another day."

"What's your grandmother like?"

"She's afraid of him and allows him to rule her life."

"Are you afraid of him?"

"Let's put it this way. I learned not to like him or my father." She winced from so much honest emotion. "They have a hard streak that dominates their existence. As soon as I turned eighteen, I left to go to school in Paris."

"Didn't they try to prevent you from leaving?"

"Yes. They told me that if I deserted the family, there'd be no money, no inheritance. That suited me fine. From my bank account

I withdrew the pitiful amount of money I'd earned and bought a third-class train ticket for Paris. I slept all the way. When I arrived, I found a job at a warehouse the next day and bunked with some of the workers until I could pay for a semester of college."

"You're amazing!"

"No—only desperate to get on with the life I wanted to lead. At that point, I took out a school loan and got another job as an eighteen-wheeler truck driver. It paid more and I could sleep behind the cab while I had to make deliveries between classes and on weekends."

"Where did you drive?"

"All over Paris and the outskirts. In the process, I made lots of contacts. After a month, I found a rooming house so I could bathe and eat breakfast daily. That's how I lived while I pursued an education in money management. After college I worked for an investment firm."

Dominic was getting to her in ways she didn't think possible. Nathalie knew he had to be a remarkable man, but hearing some of his history told her she would never meet a more extraordinary human being.

"Did your family know where you were?"

"My cousin Raoul knew. That was all that mattered to me. Do you know the sad part of this is that I wanted to have a close relationship with family, but it never happened. My father is made in my grandfather's image, which explains why we don't get along. Both men are driven and cold."

"What about your mother?"

"She's not as cold, but is in lockstep with him over aspirations for their children. You have to do it their way. There is no other."

Her heart pained for him. "I'm so sorry, Dominic."

"It's life, but I don't want to talk about them. I'd much rather focus on you."

He drove swiftly to the vineyard and pulled up behind her car outside her rental. After shutting off the engine, he turned to her. "We'll only need pickers for another ten days at the most. Since the *vendange* is so short a season, I'd like to spend as much time with you in the evenings as possible before you go back to work at the pharmacy. How would you feel about that?"

The question sounded like heaven. Nathalie's mind was spinning with possibilities now that she thought he might not be Alain's father after all. "Maybe one evening I'll provide groceries and cook. Another night you could do the same." During one of their conversations she would ask him straight out if he'd known an Antoinette. After that, anything could happen.

"I'll bring the food for tomorrow's meal."

"Um. That sounds perfect."

She undid her seat belt. "Thank you for a lovely dinner and drive. Learning about red grapes has made me feel more legitimate as a grape picker. Good night."

To her surprise, he got out and walked her to the door. "I wish you didn't have to go in." The next thing she knew he'd cupped her face in his hands and lowered his dark head to kiss her. She'd been wanting this all evening.

The feel of his mouth on hers sent rivers of warmth through her body, but his kiss didn't last long enough. She moaned when he stepped away far too soon for her liking.

"*A demain*, Nathalie." His voice sounded husky.

After letting her go, he walked to his car and drove off. She waited until he'd disappeared before getting in her car to drive home. Her legs had turned to mush. Tomorrow evening couldn't come soon enough.

On Saturday Dominic drove into town for groceries, then went to his office to do work until it was time to drive to Nathalie's. The sun had shone all day and warmed everything. On the drive over, he talked to Raoul.

"Just giving you a heads-up that I'm spending the evening with Nathalie."

"If you want to bring her here, I'll go to the hotel."

"Thanks, but it's not necessary. To be honest, I wouldn't take her to the chateau. Too many eyes. For the rest of the harvest we're having dinner at her place and taking turns cooking meals."

"Cooking."

"That and other things." Dominic chuckled. "You'll have my kitchen to yourself. Nathalie's no longer in a relationship with the man she thought she would marry. Within another week, I'm going to know a lot more about her."

"Do you still feel she's not being completely honest?"

"Unfortunately, yes. But I have to believe it's something I'll be able to handle."

Raoul sobered. "I hope so for your sake."

So did Dominic, who could see her coming up the path. "Talk to you later." He hung up and got out of the car. Whether she wore her silvery-gold hair tied back or loose, she was a vision.

"Imagine meeting you here," Nathalie teased with a smile.

"I've been imagining it since I left you last night."

She blushed and opened the door to her rental. He followed her inside with the groceries. "I'll be out in a minute," she said before disappearing into the back.

"Take your time while I put things away and get our meal started." He'd bought items for his own version of *salade niçoise* with fresh fish and rolls.

By the time she'd emerged in a sleeveless pink blouse and khaki pants looking enticing, he'd prepared café au lait and handed her a cup from the kitchen counter.

"Um…" She took a sip. "Fabulous. You're going to make someone a wonderful wife one day." She always said something unexpected that amused him.

"Our dinner is waiting."

"I know. I can smell the tuna aroma from here." She walked over to the table in the little dining area and sat down on one of the chairs. "This salad is a work of art. You're spoiling me rotten!"

He wanted to do more than that.

They both ate with relish. Being with her made him feel like a light had been turned on, illuminating a world he was seeing only for the first time. "I detect red stains on your fingers."

"Me and Charlemagne," she teased. "They're unsightly, but I don't like wearing gloves. I can't do as effective a job with them on."

"You and a lot of workers."

A laugh escaped her lips.

"Wouldn't you know one of the sons in the Spanish family working by me told me there's a place called the Guinguet that has a live band on Sunday night. Everyone goes there. I pretended I didn't know."

He smiled into her eyes. "I went there a few times in the past myself." *Was that true?* Had he met Antoinette there? When? "I presume this Casanova intends to take you."

"He knows I'm not interested."

Dominic finished his roll. "That's two down in a week. How come I'm still standing?" The desire to make love to her was going to consume him before long.

A glint entered her gorgeous eyes. "Because *you* didn't ask me to go to a place where they serve sour wine." With that clever remark, she started to clear the table. "While I clean up, you're welcome to watch TV."

"I'd rather help you." He was determined to find out what she was hiding and handed her more dishes as she loaded the dishwasher.

She darted him a glance. "Do you mind if I ask you a personal question?"

"Not at all."

"Paul said you were filling in for your brother, Etienne, because he'd been sick. What is *your* official position in your family's business?"

Why did she want to know that? He felt he was getting closer to her secret. "As I told you earlier, I went to Paris and studied investment banking. After graduation I worked for a firm there before I came home four months ago because my father was ill. As it turns out, I've been deciding on the investments the company makes. In other words, I took over my father's job as funds manager."

"I see. Another huge responsibility that takes brilliance," she murmured. "You have to be an accountant whiz too."

"That's part of it. You wouldn't be looking for a career change, would you? Are you after an administrative job and need an in?"

She flushed. "No. I enjoy my work. But I do a lot of thinking while I'm out picking grapes. So much goes into running a family business like yours. It's overwhelming to me. You have to know everything about soil, grapes, weather conditions, and that's just for starters. There's hiring and payroll. I think about the equipment you need.

"Someone has to have the incredible expertise to make wine. Another person has to know how to distribute and advertise. A man like you has to make life-and-death decisions about money. When and where to invest. It all blows my mind."

Dominic stared into her eyes. "Where has all this come from?"

"I didn't realize until my stepfather died how much went into his buying the pharmacy and making it thrive. He had to learn so much to go into business after having worked for someone else. There were nights when he was up until late working on everything. I never understood what he went through." Her eyes glistened with unshed tears. "Now my mother has the load."

"One you share."

"I'm trying. Working on the vineyard has opened my eyes to so many things. We've only had to consider hiring one pharmacist to help out. But we have to provide insurance and make sure we can afford to pay another wage."

"It's a fine line at times."

"It certainly is. Your family has to hire hundreds of workers at harvest time, not to mention your regular employees. Every application has to be vetted. You carry a huge burden in order to pay your employees and deal with all the ups and downs. I can't tell you how much I admire a family like yours that has kept their business solvent for hundreds of years. You have an unmatchable work ethic."

While she'd been talking with such heartfelt emotion, he heard her cell phone ring. "Excuse me a minute, Dominic." She pulled it out of her pocket and checked the caller ID. "It's my mother. She probably wants to know how soon I'll be home tonight."

"You're leaving?"

"I always go home at night." That piece of information came as a surprise. "I'll call her back."

If that was true and she never stayed here alone at night, the news pleased him. "In that case I'm going to leave now so I don't prevent you from driving home too late."

She looked up at him. "You'll come tomorrow evening?" she asked in a throbbing voice. Those light green eyes beseeched him. "I'll make the dinner."

His breath caught. "Try to keep me away. *Bonne nuit*, Nathalie." This time he gave her a long, hard kiss, then bolted for the door, not daring to stay any longer.

The more she'd talked to him tonight, the more he'd been ensnared. No other woman he'd known had shown her kind of sensitivity and understanding of his family's unique work. The well-heeled type of women in his family's world weren't interested in much more than his overall financial worth.

But his fear that it could be a front was ripping him apart. Was it possible she'd seen Dominic somewhere and planned to work at the vineyard to get close to him? The thought pained him when he wanted to pull her down on the couch and start kissing the daylights out of her. Hell and hell.

CHAPTER SIX

SUNDAY MORNING, NATHALIE left home earlier than usual to buy groceries. She drove to Vence and put everything in the fridge before reporting to the vineyard.

Dominic must have wondered what was wrong with her to go on about his family. She hadn't been able to help it. If Alain truly was his son, then he belonged to a remarkable man with an amazing history.

Her mother wanted her to give up on this. It was wrong to date Dominic when she was holding back this huge secret that could backfire. Nathalie knew her mother was right, but since he'd admitted he'd been to the Guinguet in the past, that placed him where Antoinette could have met him.

Here she'd been thinking Dominic hadn't been the one involved with her stepsister, but this new information threw her. The one thing she had to do now was find out *when* he'd been to the bistro. Had he gone there after returning from Paris during one of his visits home? Once she knew if the timing fit, then she'd break her silence.

As soon as four thirty rolled around, she left the vineyard under a semicloudy sky and hurried to her temporary home. She wanted to get there first and make herself presentable.

Relieved that she didn't see his car outside, she rushed in and took a quick shower. After she'd put on a green skirt with a lighter green blouse, she brushed her hair and caught it back with a light green scarf.

He still hadn't come when she started the chicken crepes and prepared a strawberry and cream dessert. By five thirty she started to worry. The thought of him not coming caused her more misery than she should be feeling for this man.

While she was making coffee, she heard a knock on the door. She hadn't heard him drive up. With her adrenaline gushing, she rushed to open it. "Dominic?" she cried.

"I'm afraid not."

Oh!

She'd just come face-to-face with a man who bore such a strong family resemblance to Dominic in looks and coloring it was unbelievable. She reeled and clung to the door.

"Mademoiselle Fournier?"

"Yes?"

"I'm Etienne Fontesquieu."

She'd already guessed as much and was stunned. He had Alain's eyes too!

"My brother asked me to stop by in person since he couldn't reach you on the phone."

That's right. She'd turned it off so it wouldn't wake Alain this morning. Her body was shaking. "Please, come in."

"I'd better not. I'm getting over a cold." She could hear it. "Dominic wants you to know he's been unaccountably detained and is aware you've gone to a lot of trouble to make dinner." She'd been living for tonight.

"He asks your forgiveness and will get in touch with you."

Dominic...

"That's very considerate of you, especially since you're not well."

"I sound worse than I am."

"Please let your brother know I understand. Thank you."

"Thank *you* for doing such a good job for us. Gregoire tells me you've caught on fast. I'm impressed. Have a good evening."

He turned and walked back to his silver Mercedes. From a distance, his tall, lean silhouette reminded her of Dominic. She let out a troubled sound. Good heavens—had she gotten it wrong and *Etienne* had been Antoinette's lover?

Nathalie shut the door and sank down on the couch in shock. If she'd met Etienne first, she would have thought *he* could be Alain's father. At this point she was convinced she'd lost her mind.

After this experience she'd lost her appetite too.

What if Dominic's distrust of her had prompted him to send his brother here to check on her and find out what she was up to? Maybe Etienne didn't trust her either. Once she'd gathered her wits, she put the food in the fridge.

After driving back to La Gaude, she flew into the house. "Maman?"

When there was no answer, she tiptoed to Alain's room. Her mother was looking down at him in the crib. When she saw Nathalie, she put a finger to her lips. Nathalie went back to the living room to wait.

In a minute her mother walked in. "What's wrong? You sounded upset when you called out."

"I am. I met Dominic's brother, Etienne, today." Nathalie launched into the reason why he'd stopped in to see her. "They share an amazing family resemblance. Alain could be Etienne's son."

A small cry came from her mother. "That does it, Nathalie. You've got to give this up. I think you should quit your job at the vineyard before you do something that will cause irreversible damage. You're tampering with other people's lives. It's something that is out of your hands. Don't you see what is happening?"

"Yes." Meeting Etienne had thrown her completely. Worse, she'd fallen for his brother, a man who was still a mystery to her and could have been Nathalie's lover. "But as I told you last night, I learned Dominic had been to the Guinguet several times in the past. I need to find out when. Tomorrow night I'll ask him if he ever met a girl at the bistro named Antoinette."

"He'll demand to know why you want that information."

"At that point I'll tell him that she was my stepsister and died before she told me the name of the man she loved. She'd kept it a secret, and I wanted to know why. Then I'll add that I decided to follow a few clues that led me to the Fontesquieu vineyard."

Her mother's worried expression didn't change.

"Maman, if Dominic continues to deny all knowledge, I'll believe him and ask him if his brother might have known Antoinette. I promise I won't say anything about the baby."

"Nathalie? He's too intelligent not to figure that out."

She folded her arms to her waist. "For Alain's sake I have to find the truth if I can. Do you really wish I would give this up?"

"Yes, but I know you won't and suspect you're more than attracted to Dominic. Am I right?"

She lowered her head. "I'd give anything if I weren't."

"It's going to get worse the longer you keep seeing him."

"I know. But it's a risk I'm still willing to take for Alain's sake. Thanks for supporting me. I love you."

She kissed her mother and went to her bedroom. After putting in a wash, she packed some more clothes and finally went to bed exhausted. The next morning, she left for

Vence after having packed her lunch. She also turned on her phone.

Dominic filled her mind to the exclusion of all else. The knowledge that he'd be coming over tonight made it difficult to breathe. Nathalie stopped there first to get her backpack. The walk to the vineyard didn't take long.

She'd just reached the next row to start cutting grapes when her cell phone rang. Her heart leaped when she saw Dominic's name on the caller ID.

She put down the scissors. "*Bonjour*, monsieur."

"*Bonjour*, mademoiselle."

His distinctive voice melted her insides.

"Would you please let Nathalie Fournier know I'll be arriving tonight with our dinner? I owe her one after not showing up last evening." He hung up before she could respond.

His call brightened the already beautiful day. She hardly noticed the work she had to do. When she left the vineyard at four thirty, she came close to a run in her excitement to see Dominic again. She'd brought a summery dress in a small floral print on white to wear this evening. Even if he didn't believe her reasons for coming to the vineyard and all this was about to come to an end, she wanted to look her best.

Nathalie had been listening for his distinctive knock that came as she was brushing out her hair. She hurried to open the door. Tonight he wore a silky claret-colored shirt and tan chinos. He carried a grocery bag.

"Well, if it isn't the mysterious monsieur!"

His black eyes were alive. "I hope mademoiselle is ready for coq au vin straight from the chateau kitchen."

"Hmm. After Guinguet Fontesquieu, do I dare try it?"

His deep laugh rang out to delight her. "I don't know. I'll eat first. If I don't expire, you'll know it's safe. But I need to be invited in."

"You don't need an invitation."

"I'll remember that." He walked through

to the kitchen while she shut the door and followed him. His gaze traveled over her. "You look lovely tonight."

You look incredible. "Thank you. I've set the table and the coffee is ready. We can eat whenever you want."

"You know me. I'm hungry now. Let's dig in while it's hot." He pulled the ingredients from the bag and they sat down to enjoy what turned out to be a fabulous meal. "How went another day in the life of our latest *coupeuse*?"

She laughed. "Backbreaking, as if you didn't know. I'd much rather talk about your day." Hopefully she could ply him with enough questions to learn the truth.

Once again Dominic had to ask himself why Nathalie seemed so interested in *his* day. "In truth I've been counting the hours to be with you. I'm sorry about yesterday."

"It doesn't matter."

"Of course it does. That's why I asked Etienne to come in my place and make my apologies in person. He texted me around six and told me all was well, adding, 'She took my breath. How did you manage that, Dom?'"

Heat crept into those beautiful cheeks. "I realized something important had held you up."

"Yesterday I had a phone call from my cousin Raoul. After living in a tumultuous marriage, he's decided it has to end and has asked his wife for a divorce, *grâce à Dieu*. He should never have married her."

"How sad."

"I had to help him with some important business. You have no idea of the turmoil he's been through."

She breathed deeply. "More and more I'm relieved I ended it with Guy. Your cousin's situation reminds me of what I avoided by not marrying him."

Dominic wanted to believe her. He put down his coffee cup. "Raoul is my best friend and always has been. Over the last couple of years I've seen him so unhappy.

His wife is making demands. I'm trying to help him. We didn't get back from Nice until ten."

"He's lucky to have you."

"One of these days his nightmare will be over. In the meantime he's rooming with me in my apartment at the chateau."

"Where does your cousin usually live?"

"In the other wing of the chateau."

She blinked. "I know it's massive, but you *all* live there together?"

His brows lifted. "A horrifying thought, isn't it?"

"Only if you want to be private."

Dominic smiled at her. "That's why I lived in Paris for as long as I did."

"But you came home once in a while."

"Yes, for visits and vacations. If I decide to stay in Vence, then the day is coming when I'll buy my own home. Raoul is planning to do the same thing. It's just as well they're separated until they go to court and a settlement is made."

"I feel terrible for him. Did they love each other before they got married?"

"He'd been seeing her, but hadn't proposed marriage though both their families wanted it desperately. One night he met a girl and overnight fell deeply in love with her, wanting marriage. But then came the news that Sabine was pregnant.

"Raoul had only slept with her once and regretted it before breaking it off with her. But hearing the news about Sabine's pregnancy, he had to end his relationship with the woman he loved. At that point he did the noble thing and married Sabine. Sadly their baby died a month after she was born. He buried his heart with his little girl. Since the funeral there's been an emptiness in him that worries me."

"I can't imagine so much pain."

Their eyes held.

"You're not a Fontesquieu," Dominique murmured.

He noticed her shudder.

"Would you believe Etienne was pressured into his marriage at around the same time? He should have married a girl he was crazy about, but the family didn't consider her good enough to marry and wouldn't hear of it."

She shook her head. "Does that mean he's also on the verge of divorce?"

"It could happen, but they have a little girl, Sophie, to think of."

She pushed herself away from the table to retrieve dessert from the counter.

"I shouldn't have unburdened myself to you. You're far too easy to talk to."

"Please don't say that. Your worries help me forget my own." She brought the two *tartes aux pommes* to the table and sat down. "I'm curious about something. Since you all live at the chateau, are your offices there too?"

Was it natural curiosity on her part? Even if she had a hidden reason for asking the question, it made him chuckle. "No. Maybe you haven't seen the big modern office building behind the chateau. We each have our own suites."

Her eyes smiled. "But you never really get away from each other. Togetherness has to be the reason your family's business has risen to such heights."

Something was going on in her beautiful head. Nathalie had a charm about her that was tying him in knots. He needed to put distance between them this evening. Whether he discovered her reason for coming to the vineyard or not, he couldn't be around her much longer before he took her in his arms and made endless love to her.

"I've enjoyed tonight more than you know, but I have some business to take care of and need to get going. Let me clear the table first."

"No, no, Dominic. You brought this wonderful food and I've loved it. I'll take care of everything else. Tomorrow evening I'll provide the dinner."

"I'd like that, but I have an even better idea. As your employer, I'm giving you the day off tomorrow to spend it with me. How would you like to cook in the galley on my cruiser? It's docked in Nice. We'll leave in the morning and enjoy a full day and evening on the water together. It's a beautiful sight watching the sun go down over the Mediterranean while we swim and eat." Tomorrow he'd break her down.

His suggestion lit up her whole expression. "That would be incredible."

"Then we'll do it. Don't bother to get groceries. We'll buy them in Nice."

She walked him to the door. "I won't be able to sleep." He'd had close to none since he'd met her. Dominic was besotted by her. "Thank you for everything."

"Pick you up here at eight in the morning. Bring your swimming suit."

"I'll be ready."

He gave her a swift kiss before striding to his car. It took all the self-control he possessed not to crush her against him. Tomorrow everything was going to change.

* * *

Nathalie had trouble getting to sleep that night. Dominic's story about what had happened to his cousin had sounded so much like what had happened to Antoinette, it had shaken her. Maybe she was losing it and tried to put it out of her mind.

The next morning her heart pounded out of rhythm when Dominic arrived at eight. He'd dressed in a blue pullover and white cargo pants. It should be a sin for a man to be so devastatingly handsome and marvelous. For today she didn't want to think about anything but being with him, and wished she could thrust her guilt aside. Of course, that wasn't possible.

She'd showered and changed into white shorts and a short-sleeved lavender top. After catching her hair back with a clip, she was ready and walked out the door with her overnight bag. He helped her into the car and they reached Nice in a half hour under a sunny sky. What perfect weather!

She turned to him. "Shall we have steaks

tonight?" He'd stopped at a grocery store and they hurried inside to find what they wanted. "The rest we can get in the deli."

He nodded and reached for several baguettes to go with their meals. Before long they left for the pier where he kept his white thirty-foot cruiser with a black stripe. Everything was state of the art. This was a world most people could only dream of. Yet she couldn't forget he'd left it for a decade or longer to pursue the life he'd wanted. As far as she was concerned, he was a Renaissance man.

They both carried a bag along the dock. He got in the cruiser first with the groceries, then helped her in, but didn't let her go. "I've been waiting to do this all the way here. I need to kiss you. Really kiss you."

"Dominic—" Unable to help herself, she threw her arms around his neck hungrily and met that male mouth she'd been longing to taste again. Swept away by rapture, she lost track of time and never wanted to let him go.

Someone let out a loud whistle from another boat that reminded her they weren't alone. She eased herself away from Dominic, whose black eyes were glazed with desire. "I'm taking you to a place where we can be strictly alone." He handed her a life preserver and helped her put it on. "Let's go below and put away the groceries. After I show you around, we'll get going."

He pointed out the bedroom and bathroom on the lower deck. They wanted for nothing. Nathalie hadn't known joy like this in her whole life. To think she'd ever thought of marrying Guy. Being with Dominic had transported her to another dimension of living.

Yet the chateau, the cruiser, all the trappings of a privileged life had nothing to do with how she felt when she was with him. He'd brought her alive. They could be stranded on a desert island with nothing but each other and she would have felt she'd found paradise. That was when she knew for certain she was in love with him.

They went back up on deck, where he

undid the ropes and they cast off. "I'd like to take you to a place I love to go when I have time. Have you ever been to Les Calanques de Cassis?"

She shook her head. "Even though I've lived on the French Riviera all my life and went to the university in Nice, I've only heard of them. My friends didn't have boats." The Fontesquieu family lived a different life than 99 percent of the world.

"Then you're in for a fabulous treat. They're magical coastal inlets," he spoke with excitement. "Great cliffs of limestone that form mini fjords with sandy beaches. We'll find one for ourselves."

"I can't wait."

"We'll head there now."

When they'd reached the buoy, he opened the throttle and they sped toward the open sea. She'd had some good times in her life, but nothing like the experience she was having now with a man who was perfect to her.

She walked over to the side to take in the incredible sights along the coast. Soon they were passing Antibes. She wheeled around. "I've been there to see the Picasso museum, but I never saw the town from the water. It's all so breathtaking."

"To be honest, I prefer the sight standing a few feet away from me on those fabulous legs. You're rather breathtaking yourself."

She laughed in delight. "Keep it up, Dominic. Every woman loves to hear flattery like that."

"You're not every woman and it's not flattery."

Nathalie turned away and clung to the side of the boat. No. She was one of the small percent who couldn't have children. The pain of that knowledge had run marrow deep since meeting him.

Before long they passed Cannes with its profusion of glittering yachts and a Mediterranean beach that drew film stars and sheiks from all over.

"I miss you, Nathalie. Come and sit by me."

In an instant she moved to sit across from him and studied his chiseled male features through her sunglasses. There was never a more beautiful man born. "This is heaven for me."

He looked back at her through his own sunglasses. "I'm trying not to think about my life without you in it. The day you applied for work, my world changed."

"So did mine," she answered honestly. "I've been so happy." It frightened her that in coming to the vineyard, she'd met the man who'd changed her life for all time.

Today she selfishly wanted to put every thought out of her head except to enjoy every single second of this precious time with him. Depending on where the conversation led this evening, it might never come again.

"Do you miss the pharmacy?"

What pharmacy? Her mind was so far away from any thoughts except for him, she was a total mass of unassuaged longings only he could satisfy. She smiled. "What do *you* think?"

He grasped her hand, threading his fingers

through hers. "I think I'd like to sail away with you and never come back."

Don't say things like that, Dominic.

It wasn't possible. She couldn't allow herself to imagine a life with him. "That's a tempting thought, but not realistic." She stood up. "I'm going to get us some sodas. I'll be right back."

He watched her leave. Whatever she was keeping from him had made her squirm, but he wasn't worried. Dominic wouldn't let things alone until he'd gotten the truth out of her. There was no way he'd be taking her back until all was exposed.

Two hours later they'd come in sight of Les Calanques. He headed for his favorite channel.

"Oh, Dominic—I've never seen anything so fabulous in my life! It's like entering a canyon of sheer cliffs with a fairy-tale backdrop. The white of the limestone with the blue sky above is out of this world."

He knew she would love it as he drove

his boat in and headed for the sandy little beach at the end. It wasn't quite noon yet. Any boaters would probably come out later when it was warmer. For now they had this piece of paradise all to themselves.

After cutting the motor, he laid anchor and looked over at her. She'd already removed her life jacket. "How soon can you be ready for a swim?"

"Right now." She flashed him a smile to die for and took off her clothes to reveal a jade-colored bikini beneath. He came close to having a heart attack before peeling off his own clothes down to his black swimsuit. She beat him to the transom and jumped in the water.

He heard a shriek and laughed. "It'll warm up."

"Now you tell me!"

Dominic dived off the boat and swam under the water, catching her around those fabulous legs. They played for a while until he couldn't take it any longer and dragged her to the warm sand. Pulling her down next to him, he said, "You thought you would get away from me, but I'm telling you right now I'll never let go."

She lay there breathing hard with the sun bringing out the gold threads of her silvery-gold hair. "With those light green eyes, you look like a goddess who has enchanted me."

"This whole day has been one of enchantment."

He plunged his hand into her hair, which had come undone. "I want you, Nathalie. More than any woman I've ever wanted in my life."

"I want you too," she confessed, running her hands over his shoulders. He began to kiss her, starting with her throat, then every feature of her face until he found her mouth. Desire consumed him as she responded with an abandon he could only dream about. They were on fire for each other.

"I can't believe I had to live this long to meet you."

"I know. I feel the same way," she murmured against his lips. "You're too good to be true. I—" She paused because they could both hear voices and laughter. "Oh, no. Someone has found our spot."

Damn. She'd been about to say something that could have been important for his peace of mind. "Come on. Let's swim back to the boat and fix a meal. Hopefully they'll go away after a while."

He helped her to her feet and they ran into the aqua-colored water, anxious to get away from the encroaching world. By the time they'd climbed on board the transom with their bodies free of sand, the other boat had reached the small beach.

"You shower first, Nathalie. I'll get lunch."

"Tonight I'll make dinner." She grabbed her clothes, but he didn't let her go until he'd given her another kiss that made him crave a thousand more. He would need a lifetime and beyond to be with her and still never have enough.

Soon they were at the galley table away from prying eyes, eating a deli salad and rolls. She'd put her shorts and top back on.

"How long have you had this cruiser?"

"I bought it five years ago. It provided me a safe place when I came home for visits."

She cocked her head. "Safe?"

"I needed my space."

"Away from the chateau. Of course."

Nathalie's pulse started to race. This was it. "Was there a special woman in your life, Dominic? Either here or in Paris? You know what I mean."

Tell me the truth, her heart cried. She needed answers now.

His eyes narrowed on her face. "Not enough to get married. No blondes with shimmering hair like yours. The Fontesquieu men haven't had the best luck when it comes to marriage, but I live in hope."

It sounded less and less like he was Alain's father. Her mind shifted to Etienne. What if Alain was *his* son? The damage that knowledge would do to his already unhappy marriage would be disastrous considering he already had a child.

Whoever had gotten Antoinette pregnant

had been the love of her life. But no matter how tragically hers had ended, Nathalie was beginning to realize she didn't have the right to interfere. Her mother had been right. She'd been so obsessed with finding Alain's father, she hadn't considered what new nightmares she could be creating.

Her eyelids smarted. She couldn't keep this up anymore. After she'd finished eating, she got up from the table and took her dishes to the sink.

"Dominic? It's getting busy. Since we no longer have this place to ourselves, why don't we head back to Nice. Somewhere along the way I'll fix dinner and we can watch the sunset. What do you think?"

For an answer, he finished clearing the table. "What's bothering you? Up until a minute ago, we were communicating. Don't tell me it's nothing." He put his hands on her shoulders.

At his touch, she trembled. "This is all moving too fast."

"Fast or not, it's happened," he whispered

into her hair. "I don't want what we have to be over. Not ever." He slid his hands down her silky arms before turning her around. "I need you, Nathalie. You're all I can think about."

"Please let me go," she begged, but he didn't listen and found her mouth. *"Dominic—"*

"You want me too. I know it."

In the next breath, she surrendered to a force she couldn't control. She couldn't get close enough to him. For a few minutes, the world disappeared while they tried to satisfy their hunger. All she knew was ecstasy with this unforgettable man who filled her arms and heart.

But when he started to move her toward his cabin, she found the strength to break free of him and braced herself against the counter. "We can't do this, Dominic." After the passion that had enthralled her, she was in literal pain trying to avoid his touch.

He struggled for breath. "What do you mean?"

"I—I never meant for this to happen," she stammered. "It's all wrong."

"How could it possibly be wrong? We both felt an attraction during the interview. It's been building every second since and you know it. I've never felt this way about another woman in my life! Nathalie? Look at me."

"I can't."

"All along you've been hiding something from me. Tell me what it is."

"I don't dare."

"I knew it!" he bit out, and raked his hands through his hair in frustration. "Why are you so terrified? Help me understand."

"I shouldn't have applied for work at the vineyard. It was a mistake, and now I'm paying for it. Forgive me for the trouble I've caused you. I never meant to hurt you when you've been so wonderful to me."

"What in the hell are you talking about? Have you run away from a husband I don't know about and you're hiding at the vineyard, afraid he'll find you?"

"No!" she cried, shaking her head.

"Are you working for some editor to get information about the family business? You can tell me the truth."

"No! No one is involved but me."

"Involved how?"

"I can't answer that. Would you please let me go, Dominic? I'm begging you."

"Whatever this is, we can fix it."

She backed away from him. "The only solution out of this is for us to stop seeing each other. Let me honor my contract to pick grapes until the harvest is over."

He drew in a harsh breath. "How could I possibly stay away from you now? Deny it all you want, but our feelings for each other aren't going to fade. Before you came into my life, I'd decided this experience would never happen to me. Then you showed up in that tent. I could no more walk away from you for good than stop breathing!"

"Don't say that!" Tears trickled down her cheeks. "You mustn't."

"Why? Let's hear the truth. Are you dying of a disease and don't want to tell me?"

Not a disease, but I can't give a man children.

"I promise it's nothing like that," she cried.

"*Bon.* I'll drive us back to Nice. But this isn't over."

After cupping her wet face in his hands and kissing her breathless, he left the galley. She heard him race up on deck. Then he was back with her life jacket. He tossed it on a chair, then took off again. In another minute he'd started the motor.

The long journey back was pure agony for her. She cleaned up the galley before going up on deck. He said he didn't want dinner. What she'd done to him was tearing both of them apart.

By evening he'd deposited her at the door of the rental. He didn't try to kiss her again before she went inside. When she heard him drive away, she wanted to die, but there was a reason she hadn't told him the truth tonight.

She still didn't have proof that either brother was Alain's father and didn't dare probe further since she could be wrong and hurt everyone. It didn't matter that she'd had the best reason in the world for doing what she'd done. She'd gone way too far and her feelings for him needed to be cut off for good.

She'd ventured where she shouldn't have and would suffer for having given in to her guilty longing for him. It had to end now before she did damage to two men who had no comprehension of why she'd come to the vineyard to work.

Knowing that she was doing the right thing, she drove back to La Gaude at full speed. When she entered the house still in tears, she found her mom on the phone with Nathalie's *tante* Patrice, her mother's sister, who lived in Nice with her husband and family. Alain had already been put to bed. Her mother took one look at her and ended the conversation.

"You're so pale, it alarms me. I'm almost afraid to ask what's happened."

Nathalie sank down on the chair. "I spent the whole day with Dominic and had a chance to confront him. But I couldn't do it because I have no proof that either brother was involved with Antoinette. He knows I've been holding back." She wiped more tears off her cheeks.

"I was afraid of this," her mother murmured.

"I'm too involved with him, but it's not too late. If I give up the job in the morning and never see him again, no one but you and I will know anything."

"Does Dominic know you're quitting?"

"No. He'll find out after the fact."

Her mother got to her feet. "I can tell how much he means to you. If he feels the same way—and I suspect he does—he's not going to stay away from you."

"I know him. He'll come to the vineyard tomorrow to get the truth out of me. But I won't be employed there or living in the mobile home."

"Which means he'll come here."

"I hope not, but I'll have to face that moment if it happens. I'm going to go to bed now and get up extra early to take care of what I have to do. Get a good sleep, Maman." She kissed her and hurried to the bedroom, but there'd be little sleep for Nathalie.

She got up at the crack of dawn after a restless night and drove straight to the vineyard, praying there'd be no sign of Dominic. She waited in her car until she saw Gregoire. No one else was there yet. He'd just arrived in his truck. She got out with the equipment she'd been given and ran up to him.

"Gregoire? Forgive me, but an emergency has happened at my home and I can't work here any longer."

He frowned. "I'm sorry."

"So am I. Here are the things I was given to start work." He took the items from her. "You've all been so nice to me. I can't thank you enough for taking me on. I hope you find a replacement without too much trouble. Say goodbye to Paul. He was a great help."

Gregoire gave her a perplexed nod before she ran back to her car and headed for the mobile home. She'd never cleaned things so fast in her life, hoping against hope that Dominic wasn't around and wouldn't see her car. When she'd finished, she drove over to the manager's office and turned in her key.

Once back in her car, she left the vineyard. She'd cried so many tears last night in bed, she didn't know she had any more in her. But she was wrong and could barely see her way home to La Gaude.

CHAPTER SEVEN

DOMINIC HAD BEEN struggling to get some work done in his office when Etienne unexpectedly walked in at lunchtime. He looked up. "Hey, bro. You're looking better."

Etienne frowned. "I wish I could say the same thing about you. From where I'm standing, I'd say you've come down with that wretched flu."

"I'm afraid I've got something much worse." He hadn't slept all night trying to work out what was going on with Nathalie.

"Then you're not going to like my news."

"What do you mean?"

"I just received a message from Gregoire at the office and came over on the double to see you."

"What's wrong?"

"Mademoiselle Fournier showed up at the

vineyard early this morning and told him there was an emergency at home. She said she couldn't continue to work at the vineyard. After thanking him for everything and handing over her supplies, she drove off. I just called the manager of the mobile home park. He said she cleaned her home and dropped off the keys early. That was it."

Dominic jumped to his feet, feeling as if he'd just received the final blow to the gut. He rubbed the back of his neck, incredulous that she would actually quit. But last night her panic had been real. He should have foreseen her flight.

"Thanks for telling me, Etienne."

"I'm sorry to bring you this kind of news. It's obvious this woman is important to you."

"More than you know."

"Is there anything I can do?"

"Thanks, but no. I appreciate everything you've done. I've got a decision to make."

He nodded. "Call me if you need to talk."

His brother walked out, leaving Dominic standing there stunned. He'd felt her fear on the cruiser and realized he couldn't get anything out of her. It had propelled her to take flight this morning. Needing to channel his energy, he reached for his phone to call her, but all he got was her voice mail. No surprise there. He asked her to call him back, but knew she wouldn't.

After telling Theo he'd be gone from the office for the rest of the day, he drove to the chateau to change into casual clothes, then left for La Gaude.

When he reached the town, he turned on the GPS to find the La Metropole Pharmacy and parked near the front. He didn't know if she'd be working there today, but this was a place to start.

After parking the car, he entered the pharmacy that had a number of customers. One man stood behind a counter waiting on people. Dominic looked around until he spotted a striking older blonde with a slender figure who had to be Nathalie's mother. She was talking to a customer in the back. There was no sign of her daughter. That meant Nathalie was probably home.

Dominic walked back out and drove to the address on Olivier. She lived in a very modest, soft-yellow Provencal *bastide*. A red car had been parked in front. Around the side he caught sight of her blue car. His heart skipped a beat. He walked to the front door and knocked.

There was no response so he knocked again. Maybe she'd seen him from one of the front windows and intended to ignore him. After another minute he turned and headed for his car, defeated for the moment.

"Dominic? Wait!"

He wheeled around in time to see her hurry toward him wearing a colorful top and jeans. Her hair flounced around her shoulders. "I didn't realize you were out here." Her normally beautiful skin looked mottled from crying.

"I received alarming news today to hear you'd quit your job and given up the rental. Gregoire told Etienne it was because of an emergency at home. I tried to reach you on the phone. When I didn't hear from you, I came to see if you were all right."

"I'm fine, and I'm so sorry about everything. Now they have to find a replacement for me." She sounded full of remorse.

"They already have, but you and I need to talk. I'm not going to take no for an answer."

She nodded. "Just a minute while I grab my purse. I'll be right out."

His world had just gotten a little better while he waited to help her in the car. She returned and he drove them into the hills. He parked on an overlook shaded by more olive trees and turned off the engine.

"I planned to phone you later today because I owe you an explanation, Dominic."

"How about starting with the truth. Why did you quit?"

"I had a good reason."

"Convince me."

She moistened her lips in a nervous gesture. "After your brother left the other evening, I didn't like what was happening to me."

"What do you mean?"

"The news that you wouldn't be coming for dinner disappointed me much more than it should have."

"That's a bad thing?" he asked in a husky tone.

"It is for me. I never dreamed that working at the vineyard would mean I could be attracted to another man. I felt it was best to leave and still do."

Dominic had been listening. "Nathalie... You and I have experienced *coup de foudre*. It makes no sense that you're trying to put distance between us when we know we're both on fire for each other. That kind of attraction is so rare I still haven't recovered and know you haven't either. Which means there's something else you can't or won't tell me. I'm not going to leave you alone until you do."

She'd been looking out the window, then turned to him with a sober expression. "I came to the vineyard because…because I'm looking for someone."

That's what all this was about? He took a deep breath. "A man or a woman?"

"A man."

He didn't like the sound of that. "Obviously it's someone who's important to you."

"Yes."

Ciel. "How important?"

"So important I've gone overboard looking for him and am regretting it."

"You mean you wish we hadn't met."

"I didn't say that," her voice trembled. "But I've been guilt-ridden over applying to work at your vineyard in order to look for him."

"Why did you think to come to our vineyard of all places?"

"Because at the beginning of the summer I learned he worked at the Fontesquieu vineyard. I planned to take my vacation around the harvest so I could apply for work. By some miracle, you hired me."

The revelation racked him with pain. He

studied her profile. "Did this man disappear?"

"Yes, as if he'd been wiped off the face of the earth."

Dominic's brows furrowed. "What does he look like?"

She let out a troubled sigh. "All I can tell you is that he's a Provencal."

That meant he was probably dark haired and dark eyed. At this point Dominic was shattered. "If you were in a relationship at the time he disappeared, did you contact the police?"

"No. He wouldn't have gone off like that if he'd wanted to be found."

Nathalie... "Yet you're still looking for him."

"Yes. I—I just wanted to know why he disappeared." Her voice had faltered again.

She'd been in love with him! *That* was why she hadn't married the guy she'd met in pharmacy college. "If you find him, what will you do?"

"The question is no longer relevant. I've

given up trying to find him. That's why I quit my job at your vineyard. There's no place else to look and I've decided to let it go."

He slid his arm along the back of the seat, refusing to let this alone. "I take it your guilt over what has been happening between us is the reason you don't want to go on seeing me."

She nodded without looking at him. "I can't have a relationship with you."

"Why? Deep down do you still hope to find him one day?"

"If only to have closure."

There were degrees of pain. "If you'll tell me his name, I can run a search by my vintner sources and possibly find him."

"I would never ask you to do that, and couldn't anyway because he never would use his name. He was so secretive I'm convinced he was hiding who he really was. I wish I knew the reason. He was around for a month, then he was gone for good."

Dominic rubbed his jaw, tortured by everything she'd revealed. "But in that time he made a lasting impression."

"Yes."

"Nathalie... How long ago did he disappear?"

"It's been two and a half years."

"That long?" He was incredulous.

She nodded. "That's why it's absurd for me to keep looking. For all I know he's been in another part of the world all this time."

But at this point Dominic was frozen in place.

Two and a half years ago, Raoul had been forced to break off with Toinette.

Was it possible? Raoul was a Fontesquieu... All the men in their family were tall and dark. Provencal. That's how Nathalie had described him.

No...

Dominic didn't even want to think it. But what if by a stroke of fate, Nathalie *had* been the woman Raoul had adored, and she had used a different name with him?

Why would she be looking for him now?

She knew he'd had to marry another woman. Did she come to the vineyard to find out about his life because she'd never been able to let him go in her heart?

If it was true, Dominic was haunted by the thought that Nathalie had loved his cousin and had been looking for him. He knew Raoul had never forgotten his love for her.

Dominic's eyes closed tightly for a minute when he considered yesterday when he'd started kissing her again in the galley. If she hadn't stopped him, they might have ended up making love all night long. *Bon Dieu.*

Until he'd had a certain conversation with his cousin tonight and ascertained the truth, he needed to take her home *now.*

"Dominic? I know that what I've revealed has shocked you."

You mean crucified me. "That's one way of putting it, but I'm glad I have the truth at last and will drive you back to your house."

"Thank you. I hope you can forgive me."

"There's nothing to forgive. The vineyard is grateful for the excellent work you've put

in. Pretty soon those red stains will be gone."
He started the car and took her home.

She opened the door and jumped out the second he pulled up in front of her house. "Whether you believe me or not, I've loved every moment we've spent together." There were tears in her voice. "I'll never forget you, Dominic."

Those throbbing words would stay with him all the way to Vence. "*A bientôt*, Nathalie."

He'd rebelled against saying goodbye to her. But if she and Raoul had been lovers... His cousin would soon be free of Sabine. He and Nathalie could finally be together.

Raw pain clawed his insides as he drove to the estate and hurried inside his apartment. He and his cousin were going to have the talk of their lives. For the first time in his, he felt like death.

But Raoul texted him later and told him a problem had come up at work and he'd had to drive to their warehouse in Saint Jeannet. He wouldn't be back until the next evening.

It was just as well since Dominic needed to calm down before he talked to his cousin. He didn't want them to have been lovers.

Dominic couldn't bear it.

Nathalie had been staying home for the rest of the week to take care of Alain while her mother ran the pharmacy with Denis. It gave Minerve some time off. Next week Nathalie would go back to her routine at the pharmacy.

She adored her nephew and played with him to her heart's content. He would be her baby one day, the only one she would ever have. She would spend the rest of her life giving him all the love she could while she loved Dominic in silence. There was no man in the world like him.

If he was the one Antoinette had fallen for, Nathalie understood why she'd told Claire he was the only man she would ever love. Nathalie couldn't imagine loving another man either.

On Saturday morning she took Alain to

the local park as usual and walked around with him, holding his hand. His little giggles while they fed the ducks in the pond delighted her. When she could tell he was tired, she took him home for lunch and a nap.

While it was quiet, she phoned Claire to tell her everything that had happened. "I quit my job." She'd also said goodbye to Dominic, but she didn't confess her feelings for him to Claire. That would have to remain her secret.

"I know you had hopes, but I can't say I blame you."

"You and Mom were right. I have no proof. But I want to thank you with all my heart for your help."

"Oh, Nathalie. I was happy to give you any information I could. What are you going to do now?"

"Start adoption proceedings for Alain."

"How wonderful!"

"I'm his doting, would-be mother. After it's official, I want him to start calling me

Maman and we'll all live together with my mother. He loves his *grand-mere*."

"Antoinette was lucky you're there for her son. I miss her."

"So do I. One day I'll bring Alain by to meet you. Thanks again for everything. Talk to you soon."

"I'd love that. Au revoir, Nathalie."

They clicked off, but she was restless and went to her room to take a shower. As she was getting dressed in a skirt and blouse, she received a text. Maybe it was her mother. She reached for her phone on the dresser.

Dominic.

The blood pounded in her ears as she read it.

I have some information you've been wanting. If you're interested come to my office between five thirty and six today. You can pick up your paycheck at the same time. If you don't come I'll have it deposited in your bank.

Dominic—

She let out an agonized groan. To hear from him now when the separation had been so excruciating for her... What information did he think he'd found for her when she believed either he or his brother could have been the man involved with Antoinette? Or not. Did she dare break down and walk through fire in order to be with him again?

While she stood there in utter turmoil, that fluttering organ she called her heart gave her the answer. Fool that she was, she answered back. I'll come.

Having done that, she rushed around to get ready and left the house after her mother got home at three.

She battled fear and excitement all the way and felt feverish by the time she drove onto the estate. The road led around the magnificent seventeenth-century chateau. Seeing his home in all its glory up close brought back the conversation she'd had with Dominic about his family.

The big modern business building beyond the chateau and sculptured topiary trees looked out of place. She studied the cars parked in the lot on the side. The black Renault and silver Mercedes caught her eye immediately.

On trembling legs she got out of her car and entered the door of the main entrance.

A well-dressed, attractive receptionist seated at a desk smiled at her. "*Bonjour.* Can I help you?"

"Yes." She could see Dominic's name on the door to the right. "I'm Mademoiselle Fournier. I was told to pick up my paycheck in Monsieur Dominic Fontesquieu's office."

"*Très bien.* I'll let him know you're here."

A few seconds later the door opened. The tall, dark Frenchman she loved with all her heart and soul stood there dressed casually in jeans and a tan sport shirt. Every inch of him was so arresting, she felt inundated with longings, but lines marred his handsome face and she noticed a certain pallor. Maybe he'd caught his brother's flu.

"I'm glad you could make it. *Entrez*, Mademoiselle Fournier."

He'd never been this formal with her. "Thank you."

Nathalie stepped inside, but came to a sudden halt. She'd thought Dominic would be alone. Out of the corner of her eye, she saw another tall, dark-haired man standing near the desk wearing a blue business suit. He was on his phone.

After he hung up, he turned in her direction. She let out a tiny gasp, unable to trust the sight before her eyes. This man reminded her of Dominic and Etienne. With his coloring and those familiar features, he had to be *another* Fontesquieu! Incredibly he had a look of Alain, as well. Now she really knew she was losing it.

His smiling black eyes looked over her with male interest. "Dom? Aren't you going to introduce us?"

Dominic didn't answer. What was going on?

"I'm Nathalie Fournier." She spoke up to ease the sudden tension. "And you?"

"Raoul Fontesquieu."

Dominic's cousin! The one going through the painful divorce. "It's very nice to meet you, Monsieur Fontesquieu."

"I hear you did an excellent job of picking grapes while you were here. Not everyone has a knack for it."

"I don't know about that, but thank you."

He walked over to Dominic and patted his shoulder. "We'll talk later at home."

That's right. She remembered his cousin had moved in with Dominic while getting his divorce.

Raoul flashed Nathalie another glance. "It's a pleasure to meet you."

Dominic walked him to the door. After his cousin left, he turned to her, but he looked like a different person. The lines around his compelling mouth had disappeared, but he didn't say a word to her, making her uncomfortable.

"Dominic, I wouldn't have come if I'd known you were busy."

"I asked you to come. My cousin only dropped by for a minute."

"Why are you staring at me like that?" She didn't understand.

"Because you're even more breathtaking than when we swam in the lagoon."

So was he. She swallowed hard. "You said in your text that you had some information for me I've been wanting."

Nathalie heard his sharp intake of breath. "You don't have to believe me, but until just a little while ago I thought I might have found the man you've been looking for. But my source was mistaken."

"I believe you because I know you wouldn't make that up."

"Thank you for that," he said in a thick-toned voice. In the next breath, he walked over to his desk and handed her the envelope with her paycheck. She put it in her purse.

"How are things going with your cousin?"

"It's a waiting game until his court date. His wife is fighting to stop the divorce."

"That's awful."

He grimaced. "Other things are worse, like not being able to see you anymore. Are you really planning to go through your whole life putting your personal life on hold while you wait to find the man who disappeared without a trace?"

Don't.

"I—I shouldn't have come and need to get home." Her voice faltered. "Thank you for the check." She started for the door.

"Just know that when you leave, there's a man here who's aching for you. That ache isn't going to go away."

She knew all about the pain he was describing. Nathalie hurried out of the building to her car. The situation had become impossible.

To add to her turmoil, there was the shocking realization that Raoul Fontesquieu could have been Antoinette's lover. The thought wouldn't leave her alone.

On the way home, she went over the conversation with Dominic when he'd told her about Raoul's unhappy marriage.

"I'm so sorry. Did they love each other before they got married?"

"He'd been seeing her, but hadn't proposed marriage. Both their families wanted it desperately. One night he met a girl and overnight fell deeply in love with her, wanting marriage. But by then Sabine was pregnant.

"Raoul only slept with her once, but he did the noble thing and married her. Sadly he had to cut everything off with the girl he loved. Then their baby died. He buried his heart with his little girl. Since the funeral there's been an emptiness in him that worries me."

"I can't imagine so much pain."

"You're not a Fontesquieu."

The same looks ran in some families. Sometimes it was astounding. The Fontesquieu men were incredibly handsome in a similar way that made them unique. But she had to be realistic. Although Alain had many of their traits, he might not belong to any of them and probably didn't.

It was imperative she put all this behind her for good.

What her family needed was a vacation. They hadn't been anywhere since her stepfather died, and ought to go someplace far away with Alain.

When she arrived at the house to discuss it with her mother, she discovered Tante Patrice and Oncle Tommaso had dropped in for a visit. They were playing with Alain. He laughed so hard he got the hiccups.

Nathalie loved their extended family and got into the mix, spending a wonderful evening with them. She caught up on their news about her two cousins who were married and had children. One of the little girls named Angelique had just had her second birthday. She and Alain could play together.

After a while they talked about Nathalie's plans to adopt Alain. He would be her life from now on.

CHAPTER EIGHT

SUNDAY MORNING, AFTER being awake most of the night, Dominic got showered and dressed. He and Raoul went out for breakfast and talked. Very soon now his trial date would be set with the judge.

Afterward they went house hunting for Raoul, who had no desire to return to his apartment at the chateau once he was divorced. They found several possibilities. As they drove on, Raoul said, "Let's find one for you too, Dominic."

He frowned. "If I were getting married, I'd do it in a shot."

"Since I know you're head over heels in love with Nathalie Fournier, I don't understand why there's an *if*. Dom—I've poured out my soul to you. Now it's my turn to listen while you tell me what has you gutted."

"I finally learned the truth. She's in love with a man who told her he worked in our vineyard, but he disappeared on her two and half years ago. They were only together a month. Nathalie came to our vineyard trying to find him. She didn't know his name, but she described him as Provencal." He flashed his cousin a glance. "Because certain pieces of information fit, I thought it might be *you*."

Raoul let out a strange sound. "So *that's* why you called me into your office just minutes before she showed up? You thought she was the woman I'd loved?"

"I thought it could be a possibility and she'd used another name with you."

"Well, now that you know I'm not the one, why aren't you with her right now?"

He shook his head. "Until she finds this man and has closure, she refuses to be with me."

"Closure is different from being in love. It's been over two and a half years since she last saw him!"

"Then how do you explain why she quit work at the vineyard?"

"Because she has fallen in love with you, but you've been her employer. She's probably nervous about getting involved. I saw the way she looked at you. After the vibes I got from you two yesterday, I can promise you she couldn't still be in love with that other guy.

"Come on. Take me back to your apartment so you can go after her and break her down. Don't lose the woman who makes your life worth living. She'll most likely be home."

Raoul had been talking to a desperate man. His advice made so much sense, Dominic dropped his cousin off and left for La Gaude under a warm noon sun. Before long he turned the corner onto her street.

The red car he'd seen in front of her house the other day was gone. He saw Nathalie get out of the blue car parked at the side of the house. Her long shapely legs emerged first. She wore navy shorts and a sailor top.

He pulled to a stop, not wanting her to see him yet.

Next, she opened the rear door and reached for a little boy maybe the same age as Etienne's daughter, buckled in a car seat. She kissed his black curls several times before putting him down so he could walk. The child reached for her hand.

That trusting gesture caused Dominic's throat to swell with emotion.

Her son? He was staggered by the fact that Nathalie was a single mother and hadn't been able to admit it to him.

Dominic wondered how she'd been able to handle being away from her little boy during the harvest. She said she lived with her mother, who was also a pharmacist. No doubt Nathalie had hired someone to take care of him while she'd been working at the vineyard.

As for her picking grapes, it explained why she came home every night instead of staying in the mobile home. No wonder she'd come looking for the man who'd made her pregnant. With her stepfather deceased, she and her mother were her son's only support.

All of these thoughts ran through his mind. Yet he wondered why she'd waited until this summer to look for the man who'd changed her life.

Not about to give up, Dominic pulled out his phone and texted her.

Nathalie? I'm out in front of your house. When I came to see you just now, I watched you take a little boy inside with you. Is it his father you're looking for? I would like to talk to you and see what I can do to help. When will you be free?

A minute later she responded.

I'm putting him down now. It may take a half hour.

At least she hadn't said no.

Then I'll grab lunch for both of us and come back.

He drove to a bistro and picked up some food for them. When he returned, she came out of the house having changed into jeans and a blouse. She looked good enough to eat.

"Do you have to stay out in front?" he asked after she'd climbed in the car.

"No. My mother is home today."

Good. "In that case I'll drive us to that overlook we went to before."

He felt her cast him a covert glance. "I can't believe you came." There was a tremor in her voice.

"As you can see, I'm unable to stay away from you." Dominic drove up into the hills and parked the car under the same olive tree. "I bought us some meat pies and coffee." He reached in back for their lunch and they both started to eat.

"Thank you. I don't deserve how good you are to me."

"I'd like to do a lot more for you if you'd let me."

"Dominic—I never planned to be with you again, but now that you've seen Alain,

I can't keep the truth from you. Over sixteen months ago my stepsister had a baby."

"Your *stepsister...*"

He groaned as unmitigated joy streamed through him. Her stepsister had been the one in love with this mystery man. Everything was finally starting to make sense.

"Yes. She adored him and named him Alain. But ten days after he was born she died of a staph infection."

"I'm so sorry that happened to her." He studied her profile. "How hard that had to have been for you and your family."

"You have no idea."

"I'm sure I don't." He leaned closer. "You've been such a good listener I want to hear whatever you're willing to tell me."

Nathalie smoothed a strand of hair behind her ear. "She was an elementary school teacher. One evening she and some other teachers from her school went to the Guinguet, a place I'd never heard of. I was working in Nice at the time and learned all this from her best friend, Claire, who lived across the street from us."

At the mention of the Guinguet, Dominic's heart began pounding like a jackhammer.

"Apparently it was love at first sight for her, but she kept him a complete secret from our family. According to Claire, her affair lasted a month, then he suddenly stopped meeting her. Two months later she went to the doctor and found out she was pregnant. I remember that she was in a terrible depression throughout her pregnancy and refused to talk about the man she'd loved."

"Incroyable," Dominic murmured.

"She refused to give our family any information about the man and insisted we never talk about him again. She begged us to leave the whole subject of Alain alone."

"But you couldn't do that." How he loved this woman!

Nathalie looked at him with tear-filled eyes. "I honored her wishes until the beginning of this summer after I broke it off with Guy. When I told him I was going to adopt

Alain, it changed our relationship. He didn't want to bring her son into our marriage. For that and other reasons, I said goodbye to him."

Grâce à Dieu.

"Oh, Dominic, Alain is so adorable and it seemed so terrible he didn't have a mother or a father, I couldn't bear it. So I thought that before I started adoption proceedings, I'd at least try to find my stepsister's lover, as he has a right to his child.

"That's when I called Claire to gather any information she could give me. All she said was that he was a Provencal, had worked on your family's vineyard and Antoinette met him at Le Guinguet. At that point I started wondering about the man she'd loved. Knowing her, he had to have been someone exceptional. Maybe something serious had happened to him and he couldn't let her know why he'd stopped seeing her. He left before she learned she was pregnant so he never knew he was a father."

All the time she was talking, Dominic

was fitting two and two together so fast, his thoughts were running away with him.

"I'm pretty sure she'd met a married man who'd wanted an affair and forced her to keep quiet about it. Since none of us knew the truth and never would, she asked our family to put the questions away and simply love Alain. I know now it was wise advice. I'm through looking."

"Nathalie—" He was trying to control his emotions. "Now that I know the truth, then there's no reason we can't go on seeing each other."

She averted her eyes. "I couldn't. Please don't ask. If you wouldn't mind driving me back home now, I promised my mother I wouldn't be long."

Beyond frustrated, he started the car and they left for her house. "Is it because of the man you'd planned to marry, your feelings for him prevent you from wanting to be with me?"

"You know I don't have feelings for him any longer or I wouldn't be this involved

with you, but I'd rather not talk about it."
He could feel her separating herself emotionally from him.

In a minute he turned the corner and pulled up in front. "What will it take for you to agree for us to be together? I didn't make up what happened when you melted in my arms on the sand. I need an answer I can understand."

"I'm…frightened to tell you."

What?

"Am I some kind of monster to you?"

"Of course not!" she cried.

"Nathalie—" He'd reached his limit.

She turned a pained face to him. "How would you feel if I told you I thought my stepsister had either had an affair with you, or Etienne."

"Say that again?" Surely he hadn't heard her correctly.

"My nephew looks so much like all of you, it's uncanny."

"Do you have a picture of him?"

She nodded and pulled one out of her wallet. His heart almost failed him when he examined the black-haired cherub up close. She'd spoken the truth. "I can't believe it," he murmured. "Alain is a double for some of the baby pictures of me and Etienne. Talk about look-alikes." He handed it back to her. "It's remarkable."

"I couldn't believe I'd met two men in one family who could possibly be his father. Then came another shock when I met your cousin in your office. He shares the same looks with you and your brother. I never saw anything like it. After you told me his marital history, I—I've wondered if Raoul could be the one," she stammered.

This was unbelievable! "You're right. Your stepsister's son has a remarkably strong resemblance to all three of us."

Her eyes beseeched him for answers. "Who would have thought?"

He swallowed hard, trying to digest everything. "I only saw Alain from a distance earlier."

"He has that same lustrous black Fontesquieu hair. You should see his piercing dark eyes in person. All three of you could claim him. When I first met you, *you* fit the description my stepsister had given Claire. You worked on the vineyard and I couldn't help but think you could have been with her."

Dominic was dumbfounded. "All this time we've been together you've thought *I* could have been her lover...?"

"At first it seemed more than plausible, but I never expected to become involved with you. That first day you took my application, I could see you written all over Alain. He has a birthmark on his leg. I saw the same one on the underside of your forearm and thought you could be the one. It's the only reason I returned on Monday to see if I'd been hired."

"You noticed that?"

"Yes. But then on the cruiser you told me about the women in your life you enjoyed, but didn't marry. I deduced you probably hadn't been with her. But you can't imagine my guilt over being attracted to you when I thought she could have been with you and had your baby."

"I'm still trying to take this in." He was incredulous.

Nathalie stirred restlessly. "You did admit you'd been to the Guinguet several times."

"So you thought that's where it all started with me."

She nodded. "I lived in hopes of getting closer to you and learning all I could first. But then my world was turned upside down because your brother, Etienne, stopped by the mobile home. You have no idea what meeting him did to me. After you told me your brother had loved another woman before his marriage, but the family thought she wasn't good enough for him, I thought… Well, you know what I thought. Couple that with my meeting your cousin, and I couldn't go on with my plan."

A man could take only so much. "Do you have a picture of her?"

"Yes."

"May I see it?"

She hesitated before opening her purse. After pulling out her wallet, she handed him a photo.

He took a look at it. "She's very attractive, but I've never seen this woman in my life."

A hand went to her throat. "This whole situation is hopeless."

Dominic's heart almost failed him. Exasperated, he said, "Nathalie? Why didn't you just come out and ask me the first time we were alone?"

She shook her head. "How could I have dared do that when you were a perfect stranger? After Paul told me that you and Etienne were both members of the Fontesquieu family, not mere employees, that made my fear worse. Then I met Raoul. In my own way I *did* infiltrate, and you knew something was off."

"True, but you could have handed me this picture. I could have asked them if they'd seen her or knew her without telling them my reasons."

"You're right. But to tell you the whole

truth would have seemed like an accusation, especially if you and the others were innocent of being with her. You could have lied to protect yourselves. I wouldn't have blamed you."

Her reasoning made a bizarre kind of sense.

"I thought... Oh, what does it matter? All this time I've been functioning under a premise that's way off. I'm so sorry."

"Nathalie—" he said, but she interrupted him because she was beyond listening.

"My mother wanted me to leave everything alone, but I was so certain I was right. You must think I'm a fool." She opened the car door.

"Wait—"

"It's no good. We still don't have answers and I'm not going to ask Etienne or Raoul anything. That's why I stopped picking grapes. This has to be goodbye, Dominic."

Before he could credit it, she slid out while he was still holding the photo, and ran toward the house. Dominic didn't try to stop her. Tonight it was more important he get answers. Whatever the outcome, his whole life and hers were going to change.

He left for Vence and drove straight to his office. Theo had already gone home. Dominic phoned Etienne.

"We need to talk. Can you come to the office now?" Dominic had decided to question his brother first.

"Give me a half hour."

"You've got it."

They clicked off. If by any chance Etienne had been with the woman in this picture, then his brother needed to know. Dominic had been in Paris and wouldn't have known if his brother had gotten involved with Nathalie's stepsister.

While he waited, he took care of some business Theo had left for him. Before long Etienne walked in. "What's going on? You sounded ultraserious."

"That's because it could be. I have something to show you. Maybe you should sit down."

"That bad?" Etienne remained standing with his hands on his hips.

"Have you ever seen or known this woman?" Dominic handed him the two-by-three colored photo.

Etienne's dark brows furrowed before he studied it, then shook his head. "She's a beauty, but I never saw her in my life. Who is she?" He handed the photo back to him.

For his brother's sake and his own, relief swamped Dominic. "You're not going to believe what I have to tell you." For the next little while he related everything Nathalie had said, right down to the birthmarks.

His brother whistled. "Mademoiselle Fournier believes her stepsister got pregnant by a Fontesquieu?"

Dominic nodded. "She swears the boy could belong to any one of the three of us."

"You've seen him?"

"She showed me a picture. It could have been one of us when we were that age."

They stared at each other. "Well, it isn't

you, and isn't me. When was this supposed to have happened?"

"According to Nathalie, their affair took place two and a half years ago."

Etienne's eyes narrowed. "That's when Raoul got married. Are you thinking what I'm thinking? People have often said they think we're all brothers."

"I know," Dominic murmured. "As late as yesterday evening I thought it was possible Nathalie had been involved with Raoul because I didn't know about her stepsister. Naturally, when I introduced them, they didn't know each other. There's only one thing to do. Show Raoul this photo."

"Agreed."

"If this is the woman Raoul fell in love with, then his life is going to get a thousand times more complicated."

"When are you going to talk to him?"

CHAPTER NINE

MONDAYS WERE ALWAYS busy at the pharmacy. Nathalie went in at nine and waited on customers with a quick break for lunch. Her mom stayed home to take a breather from work. Nathalie told Denis to go home early and she would close up at seven, her one late night during the week. It was time she did her part.

The last customer left the pharmacy a few minutes after seven. Nathalie locked the door and was walking to the rear of the store when someone knocked on the front door.

She turned and walked back, thinking it was the customer who'd just left. But it was Dominic! Her heart plummeted to her feet.

"Will you let me in for a minute, Nathalie? I have something important to tell you."

Help. "No, Dominic. I've already said goodbye to you."

"It can't be goodbye. I've found your nephew's father. We need to talk."

What?

She knew Dominic was honesty personified. That meant he'd shown Antoinette's picture to his brother and cousin. Which one had recognized her? Nathalie pressed a hand to her heart, unable to believe this was happening.

"Where can we go now that you've closed for the night? I'll follow you."

She didn't dare go anywhere alone with him. Better to stay right here with the lights on. She unlocked the door. "Come in."

"Thank you."

There was no one more appealing to Nathalie than Dominic. Tonight he'd dressed in a business suit and tie. No doubt he'd come from some kind of meeting. She looked uninspiring in a white lab coat over a dress, no makeup and her hair pulled back to the nape. But right now that wasn't important.

"Which one of them recognized her?"

He studied her features. "Raoul."

"So *he* was the one?"

Dominic nodded. "I asked him to tell me if he'd seen or knew this woman, then I handed him the photo. He took one look at it and paled before asking me how I came by it. That's when I told him you'd been looking for the man your stepsister had loved, but I didn't tell him there was a baby."

"Oh, Dominic—" She hugged her arms to her waist, hardly able to contain her emotions.

"He remembers her telling him she had a stepsister and can't believe it's *you*! He wants desperately to talk to you anywhere, anytime you say."

Her eyes met the burning blackness of his. "I want that too," her voice trembled.

"You have no idea how eager he is and will do whatever you suggest."

She shook her head. "That's wonderful!"

"*He's* wonderful. You've only met Raoul

for a moment, but you don't know him yet. There's no better man in this world."

Nathalie had difficulty swallowing. "Obviously my stepsister felt the same way or she would never have gotten involved with him. Where would he prefer to meet?"

"That's up to you. You could come to my apartment since he's living there with me."

She moistened her lips nervously. "When would be a good time?"

"As soon as you can make it. Since I told him, he's been so anxious to talk to you about your stepsister, he hasn't been able to settle down."

"I've been in that state since I learned she was pregnant." She drew in a breath. "Is he free this evening?"

"Yes. I could drive you there and bring you back."

"That wouldn't be a good idea. Give me a minute to freshen up, then I'll follow you to the chateau. After my talk with your cousin, I'll drive home because I have to help with Alain."

He nodded. "So be it."

"I'll see you out and lock the door, then let myself out the back door."

Dominic left the pharmacy while she rushed to take off her lab coat and run a brush through her hair. After texting her mother that she wouldn't be home for a while, she put on lipstick.

Her mom wouldn't believe it when she heard the news that Alain's father had been found. Nathalie could hardly believe it either. Finally Nathalie locked up and followed the black Renault to Vence.

It gave her a strange feeling to park outside one of the entrances to the chateau, knowing she would be entering the home of the man she loved with all her heart and soul.

He unlocked the door that led upstairs to his private suite of rooms. The elegance of the sumptuous chateau wasn't lost on her as they walked down a hall lined with paintings.

When he opened the door at the end, his cousin stood there in the salon waiting for them in a sport shirt and trousers. Raoul was the tall, striking Fontesquieu her stepsister had given her heart to. Naturally, Dominic had alerted his cousin that they were on their way.

Raoul stared at her for a full minute after she walked inside. "You and Toinette might be stepsisters, but you share one similarity. She is a raving beauty too."

Nathalie was so overwhelmed to have found him, her eyes filled with tears. "You called her Toinette. That was my stepfather's nickname for her too."

His handsome features softened. "When I met her, she introduced herself as Antoinette Gilbert. I shortened it." Raoul held the photo in his hand. "This is the only remembrance I have of her. May I keep it?"

"Of course. We have hundreds at home."

"If you two will excuse me, I'll go in the other room."

Raoul turned to Dominic. "Are you kidding me? Stay! You're the reason any of this is happening. Please sit down, Nathalie."

She sank down on one of the leather couches. Nathalie could tell a man had been living here. All the masculine touches proclaimed Dominic's more modern abode. He sat next to her.

Raoul found a chair and cleared his throat. "Whether you believe me or not, I want you to know that your stepsister is the only woman I've ever loved in my life. We knew how we felt about each other by the end of that first night we met at the Guinguet."

The same thing had happened to Nathalie by the time she'd left the tent that first morning. Meeting Dominic had changed her life forever. She could fully relate.

"Before I'd met her, I'd been seeing a woman named Sabine Murat. We slept together once, but I knew deep down I didn't love her the way I should, and I ended things. Soon after, Toinette came into my life. I felt I'd been reborn and wanted to marry her on the spot. Then came the nightmare when Sabine phoned and said she was carrying my child."

Nathalie nodded. "Dominic told me."

"The worst moment in my life came when I had to tell Toinette the truth."

"She'd been so deeply in love with you, no wonder she went into depression."

Pain was written all over Raoul's face. "Toinette heard me out, then said goodbye to me and I never saw her again. I tried phoning her many times so we could talk, but she didn't answer. Of course, I couldn't blame her. No one could overcome such a cruel reality."

Tears trickled down Nathalie's cheeks. "Since then Dominic told me you've lost a baby."

"Yes. I loved our little Celine, but I found out recently she wasn't my daughter."

"Oh, no—" Nathalie cried.

"It's in the past and I'm getting a divorce."

Nathalie shared a worried glance with Dominic. "Raoul—there's something vital you need to know. It's the only reason I've been looking for you."

"What is it?"

220 FALLING FOR HER FRENCH TYCOON

"Antoinette died of a staph infection over sixteen months ago."

Raoul went white as a sheet. Dominic rushed over to him, but he shot to his feet. "She's gone?"

"Yes."

He rubbed the back of his neck, looking totally shattered.

"She's buried in La Gaude. But what's more important right now is the fact that she had *your* baby before she died."

Raoul staggered backward. "*My* baby?" The man had received too many shocks.

"Yes."

"I—I can't believe it," his voice faltered.

Nathalie smiled. "He looks like you, but he also resembles your two cousins."

"He?" Raoul cried.

"Yes. Alain is almost seventeen months old now. My stepsister named him that before she died. My mother and I have been raising him since my stepfather died."

"Toinette called our son Alain?" Suddenly the pain on his face gave way to joy, answering the most vital question for her. "That's a name in my family's line. We talked about having children."

Nathalie stood up with a smile. "Well, you got your wish. I have no proof he's yours, not without a DNA test. But here's a picture of him."

When she handed it to him, he took one look and sank back down on the couch with a low sob before studying it.

"I'm going to leave now, Raoul, and give you a chance to think about everything." She needed to get away before she broke down in tears too.

"Please don't leave yet, Nathalie."

"I have responsibilities at home. Dominic knows how to get in touch with me when you're ready. I'll see myself out."

She might have known Dominic would follow her to the car. After she climbed inside, she started the engine before looking up at him through the open window. "I pray I've done the right thing. A man has the right to know he's a father."

He reached in to brush the tears off her cheek. His touch sent a quiver through her body. "Equally true, a son has the right to know his father. Because of you, that's going to happen."

Dominic's words sank deep into her soul.

"You've done something so courageous and honorable, my cousin will be down on his knees to you when he sees the boy he and your stepsister created out of love." She felt his breath on her mouth before he gave her a brief kiss.

She lowered her eyes. "You should go back in. He needs you."

"Nathalie—"

She heard his cry, but couldn't remain there. After putting the car in gear, she headed for the entrance to the estate. The touch of his mouth remained with her all the way home. How wonderful it would feel to be able to give him a son or daughter...

Twenty minutes later she reached the house. Her mother had already put Alain down for the night. Nathalie found her cleaning the high chair and putting things away.

"Maman?"

She lifted her head. "Where have you been?"

"At Dominic's apartment in the Fontesquieu Chateau. It's a long story. He came to the pharmacy at closing time, and now I have news."

"What is it?"

"I gave Dominic a picture of Antoinette from my wallet. Neither he nor Etienne had ever met or known her. Then he showed it to Raoul Fontesquieu, his first cousin who's vice president of sales and marketing. I met him at the vineyard a few days ago. Raoul also resembles his cousins."

"You mean all three men look alike?"

"To an incredible degree. Right now he lives with Dominic while he's going through a bitter divorce. He took one look at the photo and confessed he'd been in love with Antoinette and would have married her but for impossible circumstances. I'll tell you about them later."

Silence surrounded them. "Is this the truth?"

Nathalie nodded. "Then I told him he had a son named Alain and showed him a photo. Though a DNA test would be needed for proof, he sounded and looked so overjoyed, his reaction thrilled my heart. But I left to give him time to absorb the news.

"He's had a shock, especially to hear that Antoinette had died. I have no doubt we'll be hearing from him before long, unless another impossible circumstance happens that prevents him."

A light entered her mother's gray-blue eyes. "He really loved her?"

"With every fiber of his being."

Her eyes filmed over and the two of them embraced. "Darling, this means you don't have to feel guilt over how much you care for Dominic."

Nathalie grasped the back of the nearest kitchen chair. "But I do."

"What do you mean?"

"Maman—I fell for Dominic when I believed he and Antoinette had been lovers. Knowing she was my stepsister didn't stop me from kissing him and wanting to be with him all night. That was wrong."

Her mother shook her head. "But look what has happened because you were so anxious to find Alain's father. I believe you were guided."

"Maybe. But there's something else. You know what it is. I can't have children. The doctor told me it would take a miracle. I love Dominic with every fiber of my being. He says he loves me, but I can't give him a son or daughter. After what happened with Guy, I—I don't know if I could handle it if it changed Dominic's feelings for me. I'm frightened, Maman."

"But, darling—"

"I don't want to talk about it. *Bonne nuit.*"

* * *

"Can you believe I have a son?" Raoul stood in the apartment a different man since hearing the revelation.

Dominic eyed his cousin. The news had made new men out of both of them. Nathalie no longer had to feel guilty now that she knew he and her stepsister had never been involved. As for Raoul, he had a whole new reason to live. "It's the greatest news you could have been given."

"I'll have to keep this quiet until my divorce is final."

"I agree."

"Would you talk to Nathalie and ask her how soon I could see Alain in private?"

His pulse raced. "I'll call her right now and find out what can be arranged. Even if she's in bed, she'll understand the urgency."

"What would I do without you, Dom?"

Feeling euphoric, he patted his cousin's shoulder before pulling out his cell phone. With the whole truth revealed, nothing could keep him and Nathalie apart now. His pulse raced when she picked up on the third ring.

"Dominic?"

"*Dieu merci* you're home safely. I needed to hear your voice and am calling for my cousin. How soon can he see his little boy? Considering Raoul is in the middle of a divorce, it should probably be someplace away from your home where he won't be seen."

"I can understand that. How soon could he come?"

"Tomorrow. You set the time and the spot."

"There's a park I take him to not far from the house. It's at the Place des Canards. We could meet tomorrow around noon by the pond with the ducks. Afterward I'll take him home and leave for the pharmacy."

"Does your mother know what has happened?"

"Yes. I've told her everything. She believes this was meant to be."

His eyes closed tightly for a minute. "You're an angel, Nathalie."

"I'm anything but."

She was still struggling with her guilt. He had plans to help her with that. "Raoul agrees with me. *A toute à l'heure.*"

Tuesday morning they both cleared their schedules to be gone from the estate at noon and left for La Gaude in Dominic's car. En route, Raoul asked him to stop at a store where he could buy a toy. He soon came out with a bag that contained a little blue-and-white sailboat like the one Raoul owned.

Using the GPS, they found the Place des Canards and parked along the side of the road near the pond. He couldn't miss Nathalie's gleaming hair, which she'd left loose today. In those jeans and frilly blouse, her feminine figure took his breath away.

Alain formed a contrast with his black curls. Today she'd dressed him in a navy short-sleeved romper with small red-and-white horizontal stripes.

They got out of the car and approached slowly so they wouldn't startle him. She saw them first and smiled. *"Bonjour."*

That brought Alain's head around. Up close Dominic could see why Nathalie had believed her nephew looked like their family. In person the resemblance to the Fontesquieux was absolutely uncanny. One day he'd grow to be a tall, dark-haired duplicate of his father.

"Alain?" She picked him up so Raoul could get a good look at him.

Raoul eyed him in wonder. "He has Toinette's cheeks and mouth." The moment he spoke in an awe-filled voice, Alain squirmed. His eyes, black as poppy throats, darted toward the pond.

"I've brought something for him, Nathalie." He pulled the little sailboat out of the bag.

She smiled. "Oh, look, Alain."

When the toddler switched directions again, Raoul handed him the toy. "Here's a *bateau* for you."

"Can you say *bateau*, sweetheart?" He started turning it around in his hands.

"You'll have to play with it when you're taking your bath."

Between the way she loved her nephew, and the incredible sight of seeing father and son meet each other for the first time, Dominic's heart was melting on the spot.

"Look, Alain. *Canards!*"

As she pointed to some that had come close to the edge, Alain pointed too. *"Cans."*

"Yes. Lots and lots of them. And now you've got this *bateau*."

"Bat!" he burst out, causing all three of them to chuckle.

Her eyes met Raoul's. "He knows about eight words. So far all of them are one syllable."

Raoul grinned. "What does he call you?"

"Nat."

"And your mother?"

"Gran."

"I'm anxious to meet her."

"She feels exactly the same way." Nathalie lowered Alain to the grass. "Let's walk over to the bench where we left our bag and feed the *canards*."

Alain toddled alongside her in his sandals, clutching his toy. He had a lean build like his father all right. Anyone at the park would think father and son were enjoying the sunshine with Nathalie. Once more Dominic thanked providence that she'd never been with his cousin.

She pulled out a bag of wheat grains provided by the park. Raoul took some and threw them near one of the ducks. It was eaten immediately. That prompted Alain to do the same thing.

While the two were happily occupied, Dominic walked over to Nathalie and put his arm around her shoulders. "This is a moment my cousin will remember all his life, and you're the reason for it."

She lifted those light green eyes that were filled with unshed tears. "They look wonderful together, don't they? If only my stepsister could see them."

He pulled her closer. "Maybe she can," he

murmured against her neck. "After all, you were given divine inspiration to find him. Thank heaven for a woman like you who was willing to pick grapes on enemy territory to achieve a result like this. My heart almost stopped beating when this exquisite woman handed me her application. I haven't been the same since."

"Mine almost stopped too," she admitted. "I couldn't believe I was looking at the man I thought could be Alain's father."

Dominic sucked in his breath. "Raoul lost his raison d'être when he had to give up Antoinette and then lose his child, even if he found out Celine wasn't his. You don't know it yet, but learning he has a son has made him feel reborn. He'll praise you forever for what you've done."

They could hear Raoul's chuckle before Alain came running back to Nathalie and wrapped his arms around her legs. She smiled down at him. "Did you have fun?"

Raoul followed with a smile that filled his

handsome features with happiness. "I want to see him every day."

"I *want* you to," Nathalie cried with excitement.

"I could come every lunch hour."

"That would be perfect! Minerve, the nanny who takes care of him while my mother and I are at the pharmacy, could plan to meet you here. She drives a red car. We'll tell her about you. If you come here tomorrow at noon, I'll take off work so you can meet her. He's already seen you today, so it won't be a surprise for him tomorrow."

Raoul tousled Alain's curls. "I don't know how to begin to thank you for what you've done, but I'll find a way."

"After close to seventeen long months it's been my joy to unite you at last. Now if you'll forgive me, I can tell he's hungry. I need to take him home."

"Understood."

Dominic watched his cousin hunker down to look at Alain close up. The love in his black eyes was alive. "I'll see you tomorrow, *mon fils*."

Nathalie put the sailboat in her bag, then picked up Alain and waved to them. Alain copied her. Raoul walked with her and helped put Alain in his car seat. After Nathalie drove off, Raoul strode to Dominic's car with an illuminated expression of joy.

When he climbed inside, he turned to him. "Tell me I didn't dream this up. It's like having a part of Toinette back. Tomorrow I'll talk to Nathalie about a DNA test. I already love him in a way I didn't know was possible."

That was the way Dominic felt about Nathalie.

"I'm beyond happy for you, Raoul. That rose-colored villa with the swimming pool we saw is looking better and better. I can see a little boy and his father having fun out there with a bunch of colored *bats*." They both laughed. "Why don't we stop by the Realtor on our way home?"

"You're reading my mind, Dom. I want

to put in an offer before anyone else takes it off the market. Sabine plans to wipe me out, but no matter what, I have a son to love and raise. Because of circumstances, I've missed out on Toinette's pregnancy and seventeen months of Alain's life. Never again. There's no way I'm letting the divorce rob me of another second to be the father my son needs."

While Dominic waited for him outside the realty office, he texted Nathalie.

I have to see you tonight. Will you be at the pharmacy?

Her answer wasn't long in coming.

No. I'll be home.

That was good news.

I'll come by your house and pick you up at seven. No excuses, Nathalie. Alain's existence changes things for all of us. One way or another we're family now.

This was only the beginning.

She texted back.

You're right. Let your cousin know that tomorrow Maman will come to the park too so she can meet him.

Raoul would be thrilled.
He texted her again.

Parfait! A demain, ma belle.

Ma belle...
Dominic had never used that endearment with her before.

Nathalie looked down at Alain, who'd just fallen asleep in his crib holding the *bateau*. Too much was happening too fast, but it was the result she'd wanted, even if she hadn't realized it until now.

Today the world had shifted. There'd be no adoption. Alain belonged to Raoul. At the pond, his rightful *papa* had claimed him. In a millisecond, he had become a true Fontesquieu. Nathalie knew in her heart her stepsister would be overjoyed to see her son and the man she'd loved together forever.

But now Nathalie had to make a drastic decision about what to do with the rest of her life. Her mother had done the heavy lifting after Alain had come into their lives. She would always want to live near her grandson and Raoul.

The question for Nathalie was how to get through the rest of her life when she would be Alain's *tante* from now on rather than his adoptive *maman*. She and her mother would have to help Raoul with the transition once Alain went to live with him. But Dominic and Raoul were closer than brothers. Dominic would always be around. Nathalie couldn't imagine how that would work.

She couldn't bear the pain of living this close to Dominic's orbit. Though they hadn't made love, it was what had been in her mind and heart that counted. She'd pushed thoughts of Antoinette away when she'd been in Dominic's arms. If he had thoughts of marriage, she feared his reaction when he learned she couldn't give him a child.

That meant she needed to leave La Gaude and start a new life in a place where there was no danger of running into him. Nathalie owned her car and had saved enough money to rent an apartment. She *should* be living on her own now anyway. It would have to be close enough to still be able to visit her mother without difficulty. They could plan times together when Alain would be there with her.

For the rest of Tuesday afternoon, Nathalie got on the computer to look for jobs available for pharmacists in the greater Provence area. Before her mother returned from work, she'd found an opening at a privately owned pharmacy in Menton, a city of twenty-five thousand on the French Riviera. The hour's drive from La Gaude would be perfect. They needed a pharmacist full time and the pay sounded good.

Nathalie applied for it online. She believed her mother and Denis would get along just fine without her, and they could always hire another pharmacist to help out.

Knowing she'd done this much to plan out a new future for herself helped Nathalie to find the courage she'd need to face Dominic with the truth about her condition when he came by for her this evening. It was time to get ready. She'd watch for his car and hurry outside. One day her mother would meet Dominic, but not tonight.

CHAPTER TEN

DOMINIC PULLED UP in front of the Gilbert home. Today the stakes had changed. Their lives were about to be transformed forever.

Even before he shut off the engine, Nathalie came walking out to his car wearing a stunning gold-on-green print dress. His breath caught at the shape of her gorgeous figure. Her hair caught the fire of the setting sun. No other woman matched her beauty inside or out.

He leaned across the seat and opened the door for her. She climbed inside, bringing her delicious floral scent with her. "Thank you, Dominic." She wouldn't look at him.

Without telling her his plans, he drove down the street.

"Where are we going?"

"I'm taking you to Vence. There's something I want you to see. It won't take long."

"I'd rather we didn't. Can't we stay here? All I want to know is if your cousin is truly happy."

He darted her a glance. "You already know the answer to that question. But tonight I don't want to talk about Raoul. You and I have other business that's only important to us."

"No, we don't!" she cried, turning to look out the passenger window.

"That's what you think."

"I only agreed to see you in order to work out arrangements for Raoul."

"Tonight I want to talk about us." Since he could tell she was attempting to shut him out, he turned on the radio to a soft rock music station. It didn't take long to reach Vence.

He wound around to a street on the heights of the city with a panoramic view of the sea. The modern white villa peeking out from the cypress trees had appealed to him while he'd been house hunting with Raoul. Five bedrooms, three thousand square feet and a swimming pool. Everything that had been missing while he'd lived in a massive old chateau most of his life apart from those years in Paris.

Dominic pulled up in front and shut off the engine.

"Why did you stop here?" He heard that panic in her voice again.

"This villa is for sale. I'd like to know what you think of it."

"It's lovely, but it has nothing to do with me."

"It could have everything to do with you once we're married. I've been inside and think it would be the perfect home for us and the children we're going to have."

She suddenly buried her face in her hands. "I could never marry you, Dominic."

He reached across to caress her shoulder. "I could never marry anyone else. I'm madly in love with you."

"A marriage between us isn't possible."

"Give me one good reason why."

Her head lifted abruptly. She turned to him. "Because I can't give you children, and just now I heard in your voice that it's what you want most."

Pain rocked his body. "On the cruiser you said you weren't dying of a disease or anything like it."

"I'm not, but I do have a condition. It's called primary ovarian insufficiency. By twenty years of age, I'd only had one period. Amenorrhea is the name for it. The doctor put me through a series of tests. Since that time I've only ovulated twice and I'm twenty-seven. I'm one of the five to ten percent of cases that happens to younger women. It means pregnancy will pretty well require a miracle. You don't want to marry me."

"Nathalie—"

"There's nothing you can say to make me change my mind. Right now I'm in so much pain, I can't be around you. Please take me home."

Devastated that she could be this tortured, he had no choice but to drive her back to La Gaude. There had to be a way to reach her, but it wouldn't be right now. He needed to come up with a plan. Silence filled the interior all the way back to her house.

When he drove up in front, she turned to him. "What I wanted to tell you when I came out to the car earlier was to please ask Raoul to deal with me and my mother from now on. There's no reason for you to act as the go-between any longer. You've had more to deal with than any man should have to."

"Doesn't it matter to you that I fell in love with you and wanted to do whatever I could to be with you?"

"That's because you're the most decent and honorable man I've ever known." Her voice trembled. "You were always wonderful to me even when you suspected I'd applied for work with ulterior motives. Just look what I did, Dominic. I suspected three men of being Alain's father and tried to prove it. Who does something like that?" she blurted in pain.

Dominic grasped her hand in exasperation. "How can you say that when you brought about the miracle that restored your stepsister's boy to his birth father?"

She shook her head. "It doesn't matter. I'm so honored you would want to marry me, but you deserve a woman who can give you children." She eased her hand away, then opened the door.

Talk about agony.

"I'm sure we'll see each other accidentally from time to time over the years. I have no doubt Alain will get to know you and love you. Between his father and you, he'll have the greatest role models in the world to learn from. It's so much more than I could have hoped for when I started down this slippery slope."

Dominic watched her get out and disappear inside the house. If another miracle didn't happen fast...

He drove back to the chateau needing help before he drowned.

CHAPTER ELEVEN

THE MEETING AT the park on Wednesday was an emotional one for Nathalie. Her mother had been bowled over by Raoul, who'd come alone to meet her and Minerve. They planned to go to the hospital on Thursday at noon for the DNA tests. It wouldn't be long before Alain became the newest official member of the Fontesquieu family.

Nathalie was thankful Dominic had gotten the message and didn't accompany his cousin. She couldn't have handled seeing him today.

This time Raoul had brought a little toy car for Alain, bringing a smile to his adorable face. The two of them proceeded to throw more food to the ducks. Already Nathalie could tell a bonding was taking place between father and son.

When her mother and Minerve started walking Alain to her mother's car, he didn't want to go. He'd been having too much fun with his *papa*.

Raoul helped him in the car seat, then asked Nathalie to stay for a minute after they'd driven off. "Before you go, there's something else we have to talk about."

Nathalie knew what it was. Her heart sank. "I'm sorry, but I've got to get to the pharmacy. Denis is alone right now."

"Can you give me five minutes? This is an emergency."

"If you mean Dominic—"

"You know I do," he interrupted her. "He came home last night a shattered man. You can't do this to him. Your fear about being unable to have children is unwarranted when it comes to Dominic."

"You don't know that. The man I thought I would marry couldn't handle it."

"You don't know Dom. He loves you, and your rejection of him without giving him a chance to tell you how he feels about your condition is crucifying him. In time it's going to crucify you. I know what I'm talking about. If you shut him out, you're making the worst mistake of your life."

She switched her gaze to him. "What do you mean?"

"I had to tell your stepsister the truth when I found out Sabine was pregnant. There was no altering the outcome. I felt like a monster who didn't deserve happiness. But your situation is entirely different. Let Dom tell you what's in his heart. More than anyone in the world, I want him to be happy. He adores you, Nathalie."

Raoul's words rang so true, the tears coursed down her cheeks.

"I couldn't fix my situation, but you have every chance to find happiness with Dom. Just let him in. I'm begging you. I also believe in my soul Toinette was urging you on to find me."

"You can honestly say that?"

"As God is my witness. Dominic was the conduit. Don't you think she's been in heaven suffering because she refused to tell your family about me?"

Her heart leaped. Was that true?

"You've been an answer to prayer and I'll spend the rest of my days being the best father I can be to our child. I've been given a second chance to redeem myself, all because of you. I love you for what you've done for me and Alain, Nathalie. You were there for him all that time. His wonderful aunt."

By now she was sobbing.

"Before you leave, remember there's another man out there who loves you body and soul. Don't be afraid. Have faith in his love for you. If you don't, that would be the real tragedy. Dom told me it was love at first sight for the two of you. That good old *coup de foudre*. It caught me and Antoinette too. The four of us are a lot alike."

She nodded. They definitely were.

"Don't you think it's time you let Dom out of his prison? He's the reason my miracle happened to me. I'm pleading with you not to let him spend another night in hell.

That's where he was last night. I know because I was with him and felt utterly helpless to comfort him. He's waited twenty-nine years for a woman like you to love him."

Nathalie kept wiping her eyes. She wanted to believe him.

"I have one more piece of good news. My court date is in ten days. When it's over, then I'm taking a needed vacation so my son and I can be together twenty-four/seven. I've put money down on a house for us."

He and Dom had both been house hunting. The knowledge sent another thrill of excitement through her body.

Raoul gave her a hug and left for his car on a run.

Nathalie drove to the pharmacy in a daze. Last night she'd filled out an application to be a pharmacist in Menton in order to put distance between her and Dominic. But Raoul had said so many things she couldn't dismiss, she had difficulty concentrating at work. When it was time to close the pharmacy, she went out to her car and headed home at top speed.

As soon as she walked in the house, she saw her mother and Alain sitting on the living room floor playing with his building blocks. Nathalie got down with them.

Her mother smiled at her. "Today Raoul called you an angel. I agree. Your desire to find him means our Alain is going to have a wonderful life with his *papa*. He told me everything about his heartbreaking choice back then. I have real compassion for him considering the kind of family he's come from."

"I can't blame him either, Maman." She put another block on Alain's.

"Antoinette could have looked all over and never found a man more exceptional. He's so crazy about Alain already, it's extraordinary. I can only think of one other besides your father who's his equal."

They stared at each other. "You mean Dominic."

"You know that's who I mean. You never

gave up and he never let you. If that isn't love, then I don't know anything."

"You know a lot."

"Then stop worrying you can't have children. We've been through a lot of sadness and grief over the last two and a half years. It's time we filled this house with real happiness. Finding Raoul is just the beginning."

Nathalie got to her feet. "Do you have Raoul's phone number?"

"Yes. He gave me his business card with his cell phone number. It's in the kitchen on the counter."

"Thanks." She tousled Alain's curls before walking in the other room. Once she'd put the number in her own phone, she texted him.

Do you know where Dominic is tonight?

Raoul answered back so fast it took her by surprise.

Dom and I have a meeting with Etienne at the Tour de l'Est. There's been a problem with the latest batch of wine. We'll be on our way in a minute. I'll keep you posted.

In her mind's eye she knew the location of the Tour de l'Est. It was a massive round tower on the property. In her readings she'd learned that the land deeded to the Fontesquieux contained some battlements from the fifteenth century. Since they'd cleared out the old weapons and munitions from the east tower, its eight-foot-thick walls with rooms on four floors had been used to store their wine.

Now that she'd found the courage to talk to Dominic, she groaned to think he wasn't available.

She sent another text.

Thanks. Please don't tell him I asked about him.

In came his response.

Your secret is safe with me.

The blood hammered in her ears as she made the decision to drive to Vence tonight and take a look at the tour. Maybe she'd be able to catch him. After putting on one of her favorite dresses, she hurried into the living room.

"Maman? I'm leaving for the vineyard. I might be late."

Her mother smiled at her. "I hope you are. That man has brought a light to your eyes that has never been there before."

She took a quick breath. "I love you, Maman." Nathalie leaned over to kiss them both and raced out the front door.

Dominic had just left the office for the Tour de l'Est with Raoul in his Jaguar when he received a call from their grandfather.

Raoul darted him a glance. "Aren't you going to get it?"

"No. The old man's furious because I ended it with Corinne. All that money could have come to the Fontesquieu treasury. I don't live in the same universe as our *grandpère*."

"Does anyone?"

Nathalie had shown Dominic what life had to offer if you were lucky enough to meet your soul mate. He hadn't believed such a thing existed until she'd entered his world. In the short time he'd known her, she'd taught him what it was to lay down your life for someone you love. In her case, her stepsister's son. She'd risked the unknown with nothing to go on but a hope and a prayer of uniting a father and son.

Tears stung his eyelids. She might not want to be with Dominic right now, but he had to have faith that in time she would change her mind. They were meant to be together whether she could have his baby or not. He felt it to the very depths of his being. Otherwise there was little sense to life.

Raoul drove them past the winery where they could smell the fermentation before reaching the tour. A dozen cars and trucks filled the parking area. They got out and walked inside the double doors of the old battlement.

"Hey, bro." The two of them entered the vaulted conference room on the ground floor. Etienne was already there talking with a group of storage workers and managers. "Where's the fire?"

Etienne handed them each a bottle of wine. "It's always a fire with Grand-père. He insisted the three of us meet. Sorry you had to come. These bottles have undergone six rackings over thirty-day intervals and still have a problem. Take a look."

Dominic examined his. "You're right. The wine has failed to clear."

"As I indicated on the phone, it's definitely nonspecific. I don't think any bacterial contamination is at work. In my opinion it will probably clear, but it may take up to a year or so."

"Unfortunately Grand-père doesn't want to wait that long." Raoul had checked his bottle. "He's always in such a damn hurry. There's one thing we can do right now."

Dominic nodded. "Arrange for the wine to be moved. Store it in a cooler place for several weeks. All that's required is a drop in temperature of ten degrees. If nothing changes, we'll come up with plan B."

"That's the route I'd go."

"Then we're all in agreement." Etienne gave the group instructions and they left. He walked back to Dominic and Raoul. "I'll let the old man know what we decided as soon as I get home so he won't have a fit. Sophie's come down with a cold. I need to spend some time with her before bed. Thanks for coming. See you later."

After he left, Dominic stared at his cousin. "Pretty soon you'll be able to tell everyone about your son and you'll be putting him to bed in your new house. Just think. When Alain grows up, he might become a wine expert like you."

"He might hate the wine business."

"Maybe he'll become a pharmacist like his grandfather Gilbert."

"True. I can promise you one thing. I'll

allow Alain to find his own way in life, whatever it is."

"You think I don't know that?"

Raoul nodded. "The divorce can't come soon enough for me. How about we go to the Guinguet before we go home? That's where I met Toinette and want a night to reminisce."

Just the mention of it reminded Dominic of his conversation about red wine with Nathalie. Everything reminded him of her. He couldn't deal with any more pain. "I don't know, Raoul. I'm lousy company."

"I'll take your lousy company over anyone else's. Come on. We could use some noise and music." They walked out to the car in the cooler night air. The beginning of the harvest had brought Nathalie with it. Now the grapey fragrance meant the harvest was almost at an end and the fruit was being turned into wine. The thought of it being over with her was untenable. He wanted her so badly, he was in agony.

Soon they arrived at the bistro where many of the Fontesquieu employees hung out. Unfortunately, Nathalie dominated his thoughts. His cousin had the right idea to keep him occupied until he went to bed. But nothing could be done about the empty nights.

"Tonight calls for a celebration." Raoul called the waiter over. He ordered some tapas and their best rosé wine. Dominic had never seen him so jubilant. After such a tragic marriage, he understood his cousin's euphoria. But he hoped the family wouldn't get wind of anything until after the divorce was final. One word about Alain could bring new pain to Sabine and make things uglier.

In a few minutes their waiter came to the table with their order, but he also placed a small goblet of white wine in front of both of them.

Raoul shook his head. "I didn't order this."

"It's compliments of *la blonde exquise*. She's over at the bar."

They both turned around. Dominic almost went into cardiac arrest to see Nathalie walk toward them in a filmy violet dress, holding a similar goblet. His gaze collided with the jewel green of hers.

"Welcome to the Guinguet, messieurs. I thought you might enjoy the special Guinguet wine made by the famous Fontesquieu family. I'm buying this evening. It's an acquired taste to be enjoyed for a very important occasion. You two fine-looking specimens appear to be able to handle its unique flavor."

She leaned over to click each of their goblets with hers. "Here's to a harvest with unexpected bumper crops. Our family historians will be forced to add two new names to our family trees. *Salut.*"

"Nathalie!" Dominic cried as her words sank in.

She smiled into his eyes. "Drink up, *mon amour.*"

He watched her put the goblet to her lips before he had the presence of mind to drink his. For the first time in his life, the sour wine tasted like ambrosia.

* * *

With a secret glance, Nathalie wordlessly acknowledged Raoul's departure from the bistro. Then she slid into the chair he'd just vacated. After she fed Dominic a tapa, she ate one. Suddenly Dominic reached across the small round table for her hands, grasping them for dear life.

"What happened since the last time you claimed you couldn't be with me?"

"Your cousin spoke to my heart. He said there was a man out there who loved me body and soul. To quote him, 'Don't be afraid. Have faith in his love for you. If you don't, that would be the real tragedy.' I knew it was true and came as fast as I could to find you."

Dominic's black eyes burned with love for her. "Let's get out of here. I need to hold you so I can believe this is really happening."

He got up and pulled her to her feet. Still gripping her hand, he drew her through the crowd to the outside of the bistro. "Where's your car?"

"Around the corner."

"How did you know I was at the Guinguet?"

"I followed you and Raoul from the tour after I'd texted him earlier. He told me you would be there."

A painful squeeze of her hand told her how happy that had made him. They were both out of breath when they reached the Peugeot. "Mind if I drive?"

"I want you to. I'm shaking too hard to get behind the wheel."

Dominic helped her in, then hurried around and got in the driver's seat. He had to adjust it to accommodate his long, powerful legs. She handed him the keys. Within seconds he'd started the engine and drove out to the street.

Nathalie didn't care where they were going. She clung to his hand, dying to get in his arms and stay there. As he drove them to the heights of the city, she knew where they were going. The moon shone down on the beautiful site of the white villa surrounded by the dark cypress trees.

"I've bought the place, so it means we're private here."

"You already did?"

"Yes. No matter how long it took for you to come back to me, I wanted it for us."

"Darling—"

He pulled into the driveway and drove up to the side of the villa. In the next breath, he turned off the car and reached for her. "Do you have any idea how long I've been waiting for this? I'm only going to say this once. We'll adopt as many babies as we want when we decide it's right. What matters is that we'll be man and wife. Do you hear me?"

"Yes, darling."

He lowered his mouth to hers in an explosion of needs they'd had to repress.

She moaned aloud. "Dominic... I love you so much you can't imagine," she cried, giving him kiss for kiss until they were devouring each other.

Time became meaningless as they attempted to appease their hunger, but the fire kept building. Over and over again their passion engulfed them. He was such a gorgeous man in every way, no amount of love she could shower on him would ever be enough. Every touch of his hands and mouth ignited her senses.

From the first moment she'd looked into his eyes at the interview, he'd brought her alive. Until then she'd been in a deep sleep, but no longer. He was the answer to her existence.

"You're the most beautiful thing to come into my life, *mon tresor*," he murmured, kissing her with abandon. "I'm so crazy in love with you, I don't know how long I can wait for our marriage."

"I feel the same way and never want to be apart from you again."

He cupped her face in his hands. "Let's have a wedding as soon as possible with your mother as witness."

She fingered his luxuriant black hair. "What about your family?"

"I'm afraid we'll have to leave them out of it. Tell me you understand."

"Of course I do," she cried without hesitation. Eleven years away from his family was explanation enough.

"You're incredible," he cried, kissing her with increasing hunger.

"Tomorrow I'll tell Maman we're getting married right away."

"How about Sunday, four days from now?"

"If only we could."

He kissed the base of her throat, then her mouth. "I know a justice of the peace whose funds I've managed on the side since my return from Paris. Andre Godin is now a wealthy man. When I ask him to marry us at your house, bypassing the usual waiting time, he'll do it."

She hugged him harder. "I'm convinced you can do anything you wonderful, wonderful man." Nathalie could cry for joy over what was happening.

He gave her another long, hard kiss. "I'm thinking that while we furnish the villa, we'll stay at a hotel in La Gaude so you're close to Alain during the transition and can go on working at the pharmacy."

"Maman will love that."

"When Raoul's divorce is final, we'll have a big party for all our families and friends. Whether my family shows up or not will be up to them. After that we'll take a honeymoon. For now it will be enough to be your husband."

It sounded like heaven on earth. Beyond words, Nathalie covered his mouth with her own. Again they were lost in the thrill of knowing they would become one in just a few days. Nothing else mattered.

"I know you need to get home," he eventually whispered against her lips. "I'll drive us to the chateau for my car and follow you home."

"I'll be fine."

"Let me be the judge of that. You're the most precious thing in my life. If anything were to go wrong now, I wouldn't survive. Do you hear what I'm saying?"

"Yes. Oh, yes!"

CHAPTER TWELVE

ON THE RIDE home from La Gaude, Dominic made a few important phone calls and constructed a list of all the other things he had to do before Sunday. Near midnight, he let himself in the apartment so euphoric over the miraculous outcome at the Guinguet, it took him time to realize Raoul wasn't there.

Eager to share the news of his impending marriage with his cousin, he texted him. Within a minute his phone rang. He clicked on. "Raoul? I just got home. Where are you?"

"I've been in Nice, but I'm back on the estate. See you shortly." He clicked off fast.

His cousin didn't sound at all like himself. Raoul's jubilance of earlier had vanished. Worried about the change in him, Dominic went to the kitchen to make them coffee. They had a lot to talk about.

"Dom?"

"In the kitchen."

His cousin walked in. "I can't tell you how happy I am for you, Dom. I knew Nathalie would come around."

"You had a lot more faith in her than I did." He put their coffee on the table, but when he glanced at Raoul, he saw a man in pain. "Sit down and tell me what's wrong."

"Horace contacted me after I left the bistro and told me I'd better come to his office in Nice because there was a problem."

"Has Sabine demanded more money?"

"She's demanding that the two of us go to counseling to try to save our marriage, claiming she still loves me. Her reason is that with professional help we could start over again."

Dominic sat back in the chair. "Counseling? That doesn't sound like Sabine."

"No. It sounds like both sets of parents have gotten together to try to stop the divorce. Hell, Dom!" He shot to his feet, raking a hand through his hair. "No amount of counseling can make me love Sabine. That's what I told Horace."

"Does he know about Alain?"

"Not yet."

"What's he going to do?"

"Respond with my answer to the judge. But Horace imagines she'll come back with possibly a hundred million dollars in damages since our family has billions. Horace said he'll hammer out the best settlement he can."

"Whatever the judge decrees, you know I'll help."

"You're the best, Dom, but it's my problem and I'll have to solve it. One good thing did come out of tonight's meeting. He's still asking for the same court date that was set."

"Good. For Alain's sake you need to be divorced ASAP."

A glimmer of a smile broke out on his face. "So when are you two getting married?"

"This Sunday."

He shook his head. "When you make up your mind about something, there's no stopping you. How can I help?"

"You already have. Nathalie told me your talk with her reached her heart. None of this would be happening without you. We're going to have a ceremony at her house with her mom and Minerve. That's it. Andre Godin will officiate. And within less than two weeks your divorce will be final."

"God willing, Dom."

"Nathalie Durand Fournier, do you take Dominic Laurent Fontesquieu to be your husband in sickness and in health? Do you vow to love and cherish him for all the days of your life?"

She couldn't believe this moment had come. Her heart was so full of love for Dominic she really did have trouble breathing. With those dark eyes and hair, and wearing an elegant dove-gray suit, he was so gorgeous it didn't seem possible she'd won the love of this man.

"I do," she cried softly.

With a smile, the judge turned to Dominic. "Dominic Laurent Fontesquieu, do you take Nathalie Durand Fournier to be your wife, in sickness and in health, always watching over her, loving her and protecting her for as long as you both shall live?"

"I do," he answered in a thick voice.

"Then by the power invested in me, I now pronounce you man and wife. What God has brought together, let no man put asunder. You may now kiss your bride, Dominic."

Her new husband pulled her into his arms and kissed her with such hunger her legs started to tremble.

When he finally let her go, the judge said, "You may now present each other with rings."

Dominic drew a diamond ring out of his jacket pocket and slid it home on her ring finger. It had a dazzling sparkle as she took the gold band from her little finger and put it on his ring finger. The engraving said *Mon Bien Amie.*

He kissed her deeply again before relinquishing her once more.

The judge beamed at them. "It has been my pleasure to marry a man I've highly esteemed for years." He gazed at Nathalie. "How I envy him."

She felt the heat rise into her face. "Thank you, Your Honor."

He shook Dominic's hand, then said a few words to her mother before leaving the house.

"Oh, darling." Her mother ran to her and they hugged. "It was a beautiful ceremony and you look so lovely."

"So do you, Arlette," Dominic murmured. "Now I know where Nathalie gets her fabulous looks." He gave her a hug.

Alain made some noises that caused them to turn around. He was getting restless. Minerve had been holding him during the short ceremony. Nathalie's mother reached for him so Nathalie could hug Minerve. She'd been a part of their family for a long time.

"I'm so happy for you, Nathalie." On a whisper, she said, "If he were my husband, I don't think I'd ever be able to let him out of my sight."

"I won't if I can help it."

Dominic hugged Minerve. "Thank you for supporting us and for being so good to Raoul. You've made all the difference while he's been bonding with Alain."

The older woman's eyes filled. "This has been a happy time for all of us. I hope his divorce is final soon. I know he wants to show off his son to everyone."

"It'll happen before long," Nathalie chimed in. She looked at her mother. "Now we're going to leave, but I'll be at the pharmacy in the morning as planned."

"It doesn't seem right that you can't go off on a honeymoon, but I understand what's at risk here."

After knowing how difficult Raoul's life had been when he'd met Antoinette, her mother knew it was vital everything stay secret for a while longer. None of them wanted anything to go wrong at this point.

Nathalie gave Alain a kiss and hug, then hurried out the door with Dominic carrying an overnight bag.

The Soleil Hotel was only two minutes away from Nathalie's house. That was good because Dominic couldn't last any longer before he got his bride all to himself. She looked a vision in a white silk and lace wedding dress that came to the knees of her shapely legs.

He parked the car and walked her inside to their room down the left hall. Each room had a balcony that overlooked La Gaude. Earlier that morning he'd procured the card key and had arranged for flowers to be put on the dresser and table.

Once inside their room, he lowered their overnight bags to the floor and caught her around the waist from behind. "You're trapped now, *ma belle*. There's no escape."

She whirled around, her green eyes burning with love for him. "I have news for you, *mon amour.* I told Minerve I'd never let you out of my sight and I meant it."

Slowly he unpinned the gardenia corsage he'd given her. After he'd unfastened the buttons of her wedding dress, she slipped out of it while he removed his suit jacket and tie.

"I love you, Dominic. You'll never know how much."

He studied her exquisite features, taking his time. "We have all day and night to show each other. I can't wait any longer."

"I don't want to wait," she cried.

He picked her up in his arms and carried her through the sitting room to the bedroom. Once he'd followed her down on the bed, he lifted a lock of hair to his lips. "Do you know you have strands of gold and silver? You're like a princess come to life with your hair splayed around you. And you have a perfect mouth. When we met in the tent, I couldn't take my eyes off you. You beguiled me."

"You enchanted me." She kissed his jaw. "When I left the tent, I wasn't the same woman who'd gone in. I didn't know a man like you existed."

"By some miracle we've found each other. I swear I'll love you forever, *mon coeur*." Burning with desire for her, he lowered his head to kiss her seductive mouth. At the first touch he was gone. Her response enraptured him, sending him to a different world where all that mattered was to love and be loved.

The sun was going down by the time Nathalie became aware she was lying against her husband's rock-hard body. Dominic's legs had trapped hers and his arm lay across her hip possessively. No woman on earth would ever know this kind of joy because there was only one Dominic. Being loved by him made her feel immortal.

Nathalie wanted to know his possession again and started kissing him. They'd married a lot sooner than many couples, but that was part of the fascination of loving him and learning new things about him.

"Nathalie," he murmured. Suddenly he'd come awake and pulled her on top of him. "No man ever had a lover like you. To think you're my wife!" He started to kiss her again, filling her with rapture.

The room had grown dark by the time they came awake again. She eased reluctantly out of his arms. "It's almost ten o'clock, Dominic. We haven't eaten all day. You must be starving. I'll call for room service."

While she reached for the house phone and put in an order for meat crêpes, crème brûlée and coffee, he'd gone in the other room for their bags. When he returned, he was wearing a striped robe, and he answered the door to bring in their food.

They ate in bed. She faced him. "I've never been this happy in my life. If my stepsister hadn't loved Raoul the way she did, we would never have met. The thought of that…" She couldn't finish.

"I don't like to think about it either, so we won't." He moved the tray to the floor, then pulled her into him. "I've been so impatient to make you my wife we haven't talked about the practicalities of being married."

She raised up on her elbow. "You sound worried."

"In a way I am. Your mother lost your stepdaughter, then your stepsister. Soon Alain will be living with his father. Today I took you away from her. I want both of you to be happy."

Tears stung her eyes. She was married to the most remarkable man in the world. Nathalie flung her arms around him. "I love you for thinking of her and caring about her. There's no one like you, but La Gaude isn't that far away from Vence. We'll work things out."

"What if she moved to Vence? I'd help her get into a house near our villa. She wouldn't have to work anymore and could have time for friends as well as being a grandmother. Raoul's house is only two streets away from us. I'd like to be there for her and offer support if the idea appealed to her."

She shook her head in disbelief. "You're so generous and amazing. What did I ever do to deserve you?"

"I keep asking that question about you. The women who've been in my life have been so different from you. There's nothing shallow about you. You're an exceptional woman in every way, Nathalie. It means you've had exceptional parents. I see the way you are with Alain. The love you've shown him is a revelation."

"He's easy to love," she said in a broken voice.

"The day I saw you get him out of your car, he reached for your hand. I thought he was your son. There was a tenderness in the way you treated him. It was a defining moment for me where you're concerned and brought tears to my heart. I knew at that moment I loved you desperately."

"Oh, Dominic." She half sobbed and clung to him. "Do you know when I knew I loved you forever? I was telling you about the man I was trying to find. And even after you thought I loved him, you offered to help look for him because that's the kind of unselfish person you are. You even said you'd talk to your vintner friends. You don't know what that did to me. That day, like all the others with you, will live in my memory."

"Nathalie—"

He caught her to him and started making love to her again. Far into the night he swept her away. She couldn't believe it when morning came. He was already awake, kissing her so she'd wake up.

"It couldn't be time to go to work!"

"I'm afraid it is."

"I can't leave you."

"You think I want to let you go? But we'll have tonight. I'll pick you up at five."

"I can't bear to leave you, but I have to. I'd better hurry and shower."

"Go right ahead. Of course, I'd be happy to help you." His grin turned her heart over.

"But it might make you late for work by six or seven hours."

Blushing from head to toe, she grabbed the robe he'd taken off and ran to the bathroom to get ready. Within ten minutes they were both dressed and walking out to his car.

En route to the pharmacy, she clung to his hand. "If this is the way it's going to be from now on, I can't do it. Leaving your arms this morning has been agony."

"How do you think I feel? I'll be in my office all day watching the clock until it's time to come and get you. My assistant, Theo, will tell me to go home because I'm worthless. This is why we're going to need a honeymoon soon."

"Where will we go? I don't know if I want it to be far away. Traveling to get someplace will take time away from lying in your arms."

"Then we won't go anywhere. We'll just stay home and go out on the cruiser for weeks on end. We'll explore the other sites

of Les Calanques to our hearts' content."
He'd pulled up in front of the pharmacy.

"Do you promise?"

He caught her to him and kissed her long
and sensuously. "Anything you want."

She kissed his jaw before getting out of
the car. "There's nothing else in life I want
but you."

"In that case, be ready to leave Vence right
after work. I'll pack for you."

Her eyes lit up. "What have you got
planned?"

"You'll find out."

"Dominic—"

"I've cleared it with your mother."

He drove off, taking her heart with him.

When Dominic drove up to the pharmacy at
five, his brand-new wife came running out.
His heart leaped at the sight of her. Once
in the car, he reached for her and kissed
her with abandon. But too many onlookers
caused him to relinquish her mouth.

"Let's get out of here." He started the car

and merged with the traffic. "Where are you taking me?"

"To the airport. We're flying to Paris on my private jet."

Paris?

"For how long?"

"Two days. We'll eat dinner en route. I own an apartment there where we can be private and make plans for our future."

She let out a squeal of joy. "I feel like I'm in a dream."

"Before I met you, I didn't believe in dreams and planned to go back to Paris."

Nathalie gazed at him in alarm. "When?"

"Once the harvest was over. My father has recovered and I had no desire to remain on the estate any longer. In fact, the morning I had to help do Etienne's job at the tent, I was already making plans to leave for good. And then you sat down in front of me, and every coherent thought left my mind but one. *Who was this gorgeous creature who'd come out of nowhere?* Suddenly the idea of leaving Vence held no appeal. That was longest weekend of my life waiting for Monday to roll around so I could talk to you. Until I saw you, I'd been holding my breath for fear you'd changed your mind and wouldn't come."

She leaned closer and put her hand on the back of his neck. "There was no chance of that, *mon amour*, not after meeting the most exciting man to ever come into my life. Whether you were Antoinette's lover or not, I knew I had to see you again and get to know you no matter how brazen I was. I had no willpower where you were concerned."

He reached for her hand and kissed the palm. "We were meant to be, Nathalie. Whatever life has in store for us, we'll face it together." They'd reached the Nice airport and he drove to the private jet section where his jet stood on the tarmac.

Dominic looked into her eyes. "Are you ready?"

"I was ready the moment our gazes collided beneath the tent," her voice trembled.

"It was like falling into space, and you were there to catch me. Don't ever let me go."

"As if I could. You're my heart."

"And you are mine. Forever."

* * * * *

LET'S TALK
Romance

For exclusive extracts, competitions
and special offers, find us online:

f facebook.com/millsandboon

◎ @millsandboonuk

🐦 @millsandboon

Or get in touch on 0844 844 1351*

For all the latest titles coming soon,
visit millsandboon.co.uk/nextmonth

Want even more
ROMANCE?

Join our bookclub today!

**Visit millsandbook.co.uk/Bookclub
and save on brand new books.**

MILLS & BOON